RUNES OF TRUTH

A DEMON'S FALL SERIES BOOK ONE

G. BAILEY

Runes Of Truth

Book One

Runes of Truth Copyright © 2018 by G. Bailey

Cover art by Andreaa V.

Title Treatment by Daqri B. (Cover by Combs)

❀ Created with Vellum

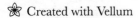 Created with Vellum

Thief. Runaway. Assassin. What happens when your rumoured name destroys your life? When the very runes engraved on your skin since birth, are a death sentence?

Evie doesn't remember a life before she was on the streets, a life before thieving to live and killing to stay alive.

When a royal family she didn't know anything about goes missing, Evie finds herself thrown into the royal court of the protectors, and they demand her help.

Help in exchange for a chance at freedom and the name that's haunted her, forgotten. A name she can't even read, a name she doesn't understand.

But when three Royal protectors are tasked with helping her get into hell, her demon ex who is literally from hell, stalking her . . . will Evie ever be free?

For all the people that live in books. For all those that live in worlds only made up by dreams and words.

"I . . . I am so sorry for this," I mumble, kissing my niece's forehead and wishing I didn't have to leave her here. *If there was any other way . . . no, I can't even think like that.* I look up at the flashing lights of the hospital, my heart breaking with every little step towards the entrance steps. It shouldn't be like this; nothing about this feels right. Protectors do not leave their own on the streets, and she will be all alone.

"We will never forget who you are, Evelina. My sister's life will not have been forfeited tonight for nothing," I whisper to her. I place the basket on the steps and make sure Evelina is covered up in her blanket, with only her arms out. I glance at her beautiful face, her now dark-blue hair, and her rune marks on her little arms. Only two weeks old, and her life is changed forever, with only her hair as proof anything happened at all. The door to the hospital opens, and I turn, walking away. I know the humans will keep her safe. They cannot see her runes. They will just think she is one of them until she is older, and her powers emerge. I hear Evelina start to cry, and then the soothing voice of a human comforting her. I pause and call (on?) one of my runes, opening a portal to my home. I know when I leave here, I cannot come back. *Not ever.*

"Where is she?" the keeper demands as soon as my portal opens into the hall. They all are standing there waiting for me. Not that I expected anything less, I had just hoped I could escape the same death sentence as my sister.

"Gone," I respond.

"Tell us, or we will force you. The child needs to be destroyed; she is a monster!" the keeper growls. I slide my sword out of my sheath, and look up at the glass ceiling to stare at the stars for a second, wanting to keep the image in my mind. The beauty of the night is a wonder.

"For Evelina," I shout, and thrust the sword straight through my stomach.

Chapter One

EVIE

"Are you *sure* you want to do this?" I ask, trying not to yawn from boredom as I hold my sword at my side, resting on it while I stare at the Protector. He isn't the typical type that comes after me, that's for sure. Usually Protectors are all posh assholes in shiny suits, but this guy looks like a fake-leather store threw up on him.

"You must die, and I will be the one that finally—" his boring, predictable speech is interrupted when my phone starts ringing. I sigh in relief, not wanting to hear that same old speech again. I pull out my phone and see Hali's name flashing. I answer and place it on loudspeaker, resting it on the dumpster near me.

"Yeah?" I answer, looking back at the protector as he runs towards me, his sword raised.

"Evie, when are you coming home? I'm starving, and you promised me Chinese tonight. The good stuff from Chingwa, not from the crappy one you like," she says as I hit my sword against the protector's, and swipe my leg under his, knocking him over. I kick his sword away from him, wondering why they even bothered sending this man after me. He is a worthless fighter.

"Yep, I won't be long, and I'll get that damn Chinese for you. Anything else?" I ask as the protector grabs my leg and calls on his fire rune, trying to burn me. I laugh, lean down, and remove his hand from my leg. I jump on him, and place my sword under his neck.

"Evie . . . what are you doing right now?" Hali asks, suspiciously.

"Err, nothing," I reply, kneeing the protector between his legs when he tries to knock me off him. He whines, before coughing out in pain.

"I don't believe that, but I want my Chinese, so I'm going to stay quiet. Later," Hali laughs, and then the sound of beeping lets me know she put the phone down. Good, no fifteen-year-old should have to hear this.

"I might let you go, but only if you tell me who sent you," I say, already knowing his answer before he opens his mouth. They always say the same thing.

"Never. I would never betray my people. Protectors never betray their blood, and we always protect," he spits out.

"I'm your people, you idiot," I try to reason with him, giving him one more chance.

"You are not," he spits out, his voice rife with condescension.

"I'm a protector. I really don't want to do this, but you won't give up, will you?" I sigh deeply and then lift my sword, shoving it through his heart before he can reply. His mouth widens in shock as I pull my sword out and stand up.

"Death *will* find you. We will never stop hunting you," he breathes out, just before his soul light leaves his body, floating up into the sky. I remember the first time I had to kill a protector, and I saw the light of his soul leave his body. It scared me, but then I saw it as what it truly is, beautiful. Beautiful that even an evil protector has light in his soul. That no matter how many of my own people I am forced to kill to survive, there might be a little bit of light remaining in my own soul. *At least I can hope there is.*

"If only things could be different," I say, disappointed in yet another one of my kind. Pulling the pen and little notebook from my pocket that I carry everywhere with me now, I flip it open and rip out a page. I quickly jot down the same thing I do every time I am forced to kill those that come after me . . . my rune name. It is the very reason I am hunted, the thing that many people now fear, and yet, I have no idea what it actually says. I leave the note on his stomach and pick my phone up before walking out of the alleyway, down the empty street.

"Crappy Chinese, here I come," I mutter, wishing Hali didn't love that place. They don't do the bacon fried rice that I love, or anything with bacon in it. The place sucks. I keep my eyes down as I walk down the empty streets of the small Scottish town where I live. The people here don't come out after dark, too scared of the possibility that demons are around. Little do they know that demons wouldn't be interested in a small town like this. It's why I chose to live here. The flashing lights of the Chinese place come into view, and I walk across the road, pulling the door open and hearing the ringing of the little bell. The middle-aged Chinese woman looks up, rolls her eyes at me, and looks back down.

"Hello to you, too," I mutter, but the woman doesn't reply to me. I grab a Chinese menu off the side, flipping through it before looking back at the woman.

"I'm ready to order," I say, trying to get her attention.

"Your child called and placed your order already, Evie."

"She isn't my child, more like a pain in my ass. I'll just wait then," I grumble, putting the menu back in its place.

"A young girl like you shouldn't be out on the streets at night," the woman says, stopping me from walking away.

"Thank you for your concern, but I'm not afraid of demons."

"No, your kind is never afraid of what they hunt," she chuckles, as the bell rings behind her. She walks over to get my bag of food before I can reply to her. Not many beings can sense what I am, and I'm quite surprised a human had the ability. She hands the bag over the counter to me.

"How did you know?" I ask.

"My family have always been able to sense things. You should be careful at night, Miss Evie. Demons are not what *you* should fear." With those cryptic words she walks away, leaving me standing in the shop alone and wondering if she is mad, or possibly, telling me the truth.

Chapter Two

EVIE

"Awesome, you're finally back," Hali says, coming out of the kitchen, and running over to me. She doesn't look at me with any kind of care or worry, nope her eyes are just on the Chinese. *A girl after my own heart, right there.*

"I have to feed the teenager I look after, don't I?" I say, and she smiles, taking the bag off me. I glance over at Hali, wondering when she started to look so much older. She doesn't look like a child anymore, which to be honest with myself, freaks me out a little. She turned fifteen yesterday, but I still think of her as the eight-year-old she was when she started living with me, after her mother died. Hali is beautiful, with black, long African hair which she braids, and it matches her deep-brown skin. She has stunning pale-grey eyes, that all witches have, and nearly all lights reflect off them. I turn around, pulling my coat off and hanging it on the hook by the front door. I put my sword underneath it, using my coat to hide the blood on it from Hali. I catch a glimpse of myself in the mirror behind the door, almost cringing at how much of a mess I am. My dark-blue, waist length hair is messy today, and my blue eyes look tired. I don't look like my twenty-five-year-old age, no, I look about fifty from all the stress. *I swear if I find a grey hair, I'm going to lose it.*

"Did you finally kill the Protector following you?" Hali asks, shocking me as she sits on the sofa and pulls Chinese boxes out of the bag like she didn't just ask something important.

"How did you even know we had one following?" I ask, curious. She never has noticed before, and she is basically a human until she turns eighteen, so it couldn't be magic she used to find out.

"You look tired, exhausted really, and it's because you don't sleep when one follows us. Plus, you have blood on your boots," she says, and I look down, seeing that she is right. *Damn, I hope that comes off, these are new boots.* I reach over, picking up a box and grabbing a plastic fork out of the bag.

"Good work, detective," I say, making her

laugh, but it dies off quickly as her pale, serious eyes meet mine.

"Do you think they will ever stop coming after you? What did you do anyway?" she asks, and I go to change the subject because she is too young to deal with the truth, when she interrupts me.

"Don't lie to me. I'm not a kid anymore, and don't you think I have a right to know?" she asks, locking her eyes with mine, so I can't really look away. I know she isn't a child, sort of, but I still want to protect her. She is like a little sister to me, and the only person in the world I'm close with. I don't want her to understand the evil in this world until she really has to. This world is full of demons, protectors, witches, angels, and even the occasional reaper. It was, apparently, better a hundred years ago when all supes used to hide from humans. Now everyone knows about supes, and supes rule the very world humans pretend they still have control over.

"They don't come for you, so no, not really," I say, shoving food into my mouth, hoping she will just drop this. I almost gag on the taste of the sweet and sour chicken, it's crap. *I miss bacon already.*

"Evie . . . protectors don't come after me now, but you know I will be hunted when I'm older. It's why you teach me how to fight, and it's why we live in the middle of Scotland. I want to know why they come after you, as you already know why they will surely come after me," she says, seeming much older than she should. I've always known why they will come after Hali one day, but I won't let anyone touch her.

"I don't know why they come after me, Hali, but I know they can find me because of my rune name. Protectors can always find one another if they know their rune name," I explain to her the little I actually do know. I don't even want to think about my asshole ex who is the only reason I know this much about my own kind.

"Like a tracker?" she asks, thinking about it. "Why don't you just remove the rune name off your skin? It doesn't give you powers like your others."

"The problem is, I don't even know what my rune name says, and have no clue how anyone else could know it. I won't remove it, not until I know. I was born with it, and whether it's a curse or not, it's mine. It's the only potential answer I have to my past, and one day I will find out what it says," I explain to her, and her eyes cloud over in sadness. I often forget what she was born with herself, and how she lost everything because of it.

"Could it be your family that knows? That send their people to kill you?" she asks.

"I don't have any family, not other than you," I reply quickly.

"I mean blood family. You had to have had a mother and father, and it would make sense they would know your rune name," she says.

"I don't get why the person hunting me doesn't just come after me themself, but that's not your problem," I say. "Now let's change the subject to something less depressing."

"Like watching the new Catfish episodes?" she says, thankfully agreeing to the subject change, despite the sadness I still see in her eyes. I smile at the big, fake grin on her face. She is hooked on these shows, and I can't say I don't find them funny and addictive as well.

"Go on, then," I say, smiling at her overly excited face as she grabs the remote.

Chapter Three

EVIE

"Faster. You need to hit that quicker and jump a tad higher next time," I warn Hali, and she nods, listening to me for once. That's a surprise; since she became a teenager, she's stopped listening like her ears fell off or something. I watch as she steps back, runs, and jumps in the air, while throwing her dagger at the same time at the moving targets. She hits one dead in the centre. *That's my girl.* I hold my hand up, high-fiving her before picking my own daggers up. "Perfect!"

"It only took five tries," she says proudly, and I pat her shoulder. It would have been two attempts if she'd listened to me the first time I offered her advice.

"How's school?" I ask her as she sits down on

the bench. I glance at the other five demons in the training room at a local private gym, each training their demon children. It's the only safe place to train around here, even if the demons act scared of us. Well, more like scared of Hali. They know what she is, and that she shouldn't be training with demons or me.

"Crap, as usual," she claims and rolls her eyes at me. I step onto the marked 'x' and hold my dagger up. Keeping my eyes on the moving targets, I throw one and hit the head of the target perfectly.

"Come on, there must be more," I push her for more of an answer, and she sighs.

"Fine. The human kids are crap to me because they know I'm not one of them, and all of the supes just ignore me. I basically go to class, eat lunch alone, and then come back home," she says. I pause at her lost, lonely tone, putting the daggers down, and going to sit next to her. I bump her shoulder, making her look at me like I'm mad.

"You don't need friends, you have me," I respond with the only thing I can think of. I didn't go to school, so I don't have a clue what she is going through. I do know she can't leave that school. It's the only place there are no witches, and no one to notice her. It's safe there for her, and I won't be able to find another school like it. It's why we live in a sleepy Scotland town, just outside of Inverness. Inverness is busy enough that no one really notices me and Hali when we come here to train and buy stuff.

"But you're too *old* to be my friend," the cheeky little shit replies. I ruffle her hair, making her laugh. I allow her to push me away before putting my arm around her shoulder and pulling her to me for a hug.

"I'm not old, so don't try that with me. I know school's shit, but people are like that. It's best you learn it now and not later," I say, and she sighs, hugging me tightly for a second before standing up.

"I know that, but it still doesn't change that I get lonely sometimes. I don't really have a future to look forward to," she says, turning around, and walking away quickly. I want to tell her she does, but lying to her never feels right. She is growing up, and it's hard to accept. I pick up two of the daggers, when I hear a shout, and then a loud gunshot followed by a scream. Just as another scream fills the training room, I turn around and see an alleyway door open. The noise seems to be coming from there/that direction. The demons all run away as I run straight towards the door. Slipping outside, I find a dead male demon on the ground with a gunshot hole where his heart should be. Then I see the two men holding a struggling young demon woman between them. They are pushing her into the wall and ripping her clothes as she screams. Blood pours down from a cut on her forehead, and her petrified eyes meet mine before she mouths "help".

"Oi! Assholes!" I shout, making the men turn towards me.

"You want to join in, demon bitch?" the man on the right says in a thick Scottish accent. Honestly, I can barely understand the idiot. Their gun is on the floor next to the dead demon. They must have dropped it...seriously bad move. I purposefully step on it as I move forward, making it clear that it's now mine. I look at both of them slowly, realising they are just humans. Ugly and clearly stupid ones at that. I glance back at the demon, taking in her pink skin and red hair. I would guess she is a succubus demon. Human men can't resist them and will lose their minds over one if they get too close. *She shouldn't be out on the streets, so why is she?*

"I will count to ten. When I get to five, if you're still here, I *will* stab you. If you still haven't run away by the time I get to ten...well, I will be chopping *other* parts off," I purposely look at where I'm thinking of chopping as I spin the daggers in my hands.

"One," is all I need to say before they turn and run away. *Cowards.* The demon woman crawls across the floor, picking up the man's head and placing it in her lap.

"Don't die, please. I need you," she pleads as she starts to sob, resting her forehead against his. I don't want to interrupt, so I pick the gun up and empty the chamber of the bullets inside before snapping the gun in two and throwing the pieces away.

"You should leave, the humans could come back any moment," I eventually say to the succubus demon.

"I don't have anywhere to go. I lived in a demon compound in Spain, but it was raided and destroyed. We came here because we heard there might be somewhere safe, but it's even worse. I can't live around humans, so what am I supposed to do? I might as well just die with him rather than going back to Hell," she says, breaking into sobs once again.

"I can take you somewhere safe, with other demons, and the humans there are in relationships with demons, so they won't hurt you. We have to leave now. The human police will come soon, and we don't want to be here for that," I tell her. They will kill her, and me, for disturbing the peace. She nods, shakily standing up and walking over to me. She follows me into the training room, and I close the doors behind us.

"Evie?" Hali's quiet voice comes from behind me. I turn to see her looking at the succubus demon, and then back to me.

"She needs to go to you know where. Get the car started, Hali," I chuck her the keys from my back pocket, and she nods, running to the entrance and out the doors.

"Can I trust you? Are you a demon?" she asks, clearly guessing demon because of my blue hair. My blue hair let me fit in with them when I was younger and helped hide me.

"You can trust me, but I'm no demon. I'm not going to lie to you," I say, and she pauses, giving me a anxious look. I walk to the entrance, seeing the other demons near the door shooting me nervous looks.

"She is the assassin. The one we all hear whispers about," one of the other demons says, fear creeping into his voice.

"Then you will know to stay silent about her mate, and what happened here. You never saw us," I tell them all and they all look away, tense and uneasy. I know they won't speak, but we can't come back to train here anymore. I look back at the succubus demon still standing behind me.

"Are you coming or not?" I ask, knowing I don't have a lot of time before the police arrive. Or worse, protectors.

"Yes. I've heard of you, and you protect demons. At least, that's what they say," she says quietly, walking out the door with me.

"I protect people like you, that had no choice. Nothing more," I tell her firmly.

"But to us . . . it is something that no one else freely gives, and demons never forget," she says. I immediately spot Hali and my car right out in front of the car park; my old Rover is hard to miss with its dirt-covered hood and the awful noise it makes. I'm surprised it still works, considering I can't remember the last time I took it to a garage. The succubus demon climbs in the back as Hali slides over to the passenger seat, and I get in the driver's. I frown when Hali hands me a red rose, with a small white note attached to it.

"Where did you find this?" I demand.

"On the wheel," she replies, and I grit my teeth as I open the note. It doesn't say anything, there's just an 'A' written on it. I open my window, chucking it out before winding my window back up.

"Why do you throw such a lovely gift away?" the succubus demon asks.

"When the sender is your ex, and he is pure evil. Literally," I say, and her eyes widen as she sits back in her seat, and I turn around. Hali whacks my arm, huffing.

"Azi isn't evil," she exclaims.

"Don't," I warn her, and she sits back with a scowl on her face as I start the car and drive off.

Chapter Four

EVIE

"I'M GOING TO BE BACK LATE TONIGHT. YOU WILL need to get your own dinner," I tell Hali, who nods as she picks up her bag. I look out the window at the foggy morning, not even able to see the end of the street as the fog is so bad. I finish the last of my bacon sandwich, before putting the empty plate in the sink.

"Work?" she asks as she grabs a drink and some fruit off the side. When she finally looks at me, the disappointment I heard in her voice is reflected in her eyes as well.

"We have to survive somehow, so don't look at me like that," I roll my eyes at her.

"But killing demons for money? How is that right?" she asks me.

"I don't kill *good* demons, if there even is such a thing. I've explained all this to you a dozen times, Hali," I tell her.

"Yes, I know you have. Demons come to Earth all the time. Protectors send any back to Hell that break the laws. The ones allowed to live still do bad things in secret, and you have to stop them, blah, blah, blah." She leans against the door, "But, you aren't a protector, and I'm scared one of those demons you go after is going to kill you before you can kill them. You go after the evil ones, and they do, well, evil things."

"Don't worry about me. I know what I'm doing," I say, ignoring the annoyed stare she gives me.

"I know you're fast, and you're powerful, but you don't have anyone to save you when things get rough. You need that, or you need to stop going after demons for money." She gives me a slightly sad smile before opening the front door, though I don't have a reply for her. Killing demons is all I know, all I've *ever* known. I was trained to do that, and it's a damn sight better than being a thief like I used to be when I was a kid. I can't tell Hali any of that. I can't even explain what the demon has done, or why I'm going to kill him tonight. Let's just say he deserves to go back to Hell.

"Contacts! You forgot to put your contacts in!" I shout, just before she can shut the door, and she pushes it open again.

"Crap," she mutters, running to her room. I grab my coat, clipping my daggers into place underneath it and sliding my other daggers into my knee-high boots. After pulling my hair up into a high ponytail, I hear Hali shutting the door as she leaves without saying goodbye. I pull my phone out, checking the address of the club the demon will be at just as I hear a slight clicking noise. I lift my head, searching for the unfamiliar noise, but not hearing anything else as I slide my phone back into my pocket. Only seconds later, I hear a loud scream, a scream I recognise. I run out the door, jumping down the stairs, and slamming the door open.

"Evie . . .," Hali cries out, as I stop just outside the door in slight shock. I keep my face calm when I see five Protectors in hoods, one of them holding Hali with a dagger pressed against her throat. I can't see the faces of any of the Protectors, only the black hoods covering them, and the Protector symbol on their hood to mark who they are. Their cloaks sway in the breeze, in the silence of the empty street.

"You will come with us," the Protector on the far right says in a deep voice. I chuckle, reaching into my cloak and sliding out a dagger as I weigh up my options. Five against one, not fair, but not impossible.

"I really don't think so," I reply simply. Hali cries as the Protector holding her bends her head forward, pulling her hair up, and showing me the witch mark on the back of her head.

"A witch mark . . . a mark that indicates she will kill a royal witch. She is a monster, and yet you still protect her?" the Protector holding her says, lifting his head, but I cannot see his face under the large hood.

"A mark doesn't make her a monster. Now, let her go, or I will show you what a monster *really* is," I say, twirling my dagger in my hand.

"This mark means she must be killed, and no law would stop us. You will come with us, with no fight, or we will kill the witch," the man holding her says, and his cloak hood falls down. His white eyes meet mine, matching his white hair. He is much older than I thought he would be, with a wrinkled face and old eyes. Protectors don't age like humans, or even like witches. We live for thousands of years. I've heard it takes two thousand years before your hair and eyes lose all colour. It's a sign you are near your end.

"Or I could just kill you all?" I ask, with large smile.

"You won't be able to get to her before I slit her throat. I have killed thousands of witches, demons, and even an angel once . . . . Do not test me, child," he says, and I believe every word in his cold stare. I lock my eyes with his as he pulls Hali's head back up, still holding the dagger in his other hand. I've seen the faces of killers, ones who will never stop until they get what they want. Ones who have killed so many that death means nothing to them anymore, and his is one of them. I will have to come up with another plan, but for now, it seems going with them is the only option. They clearly want something from me. I carefully roll my eyes over the four other Protectors here, seeing their big builds, the shine of their swords under their cloaks. I will need to take them out slowly, one by one. Not all at once. And then I could portal me and Hali out of here.

"Fine, but you let her go now," I demand, dropping my dagger on the floor. I can't fight my way out of this, not without Hali getting hurt. I won't let them do that, she is all I have.

"The girl comes with us," the Protector says, moving the dagger away from Hali and nodding his head at the Protector on his left. The Protector walks up to me, pulling out two small silver wrist bands.

"Wear them, now. We know you can portal like us," the Protector says, and I look over at Hali who shakes her head forcefully.

"Don't, Evie. Run!" she pleads with me, but one look at the Protector holding her, and I know me running would cost Hali her life. A life she hasn't even gotten to live. I'm twenty-five. I've had more years than she has, and this is my past catching up to me. I hold my hands out, and the protector snaps the silver bands on both my wrists. They burn instead of feeling cold like I thought they would, sending a fire-like feeling straight up my arms, and my four runes burn like crazy.

"Fucking hell, this is why I'm not into bondage," I grit out, making the Protector who cuffed me laugh a little.

"Connor, take her to the car," the Protector

holding Hali says. Connor goes to grab my arm, and I step back.

"I can walk to the car. You don't need to pull me like some caveman," I say, walking forward, with Connor following me, still lightly chuckling. *Damn, he has a sexy chuckle, and that's not what I need to be thinking about.* I keep my eyes on the Protectors as drag Hali into a different car, shutting the door behind them, and the car takes off silently. Three Protectors stay near me, one opening the door to a sleek, black Mercedes. I slide in, watching the door shut behind me, and two of the Protectors get into the front seats as the last protector opens a portal. No doubt he is going ahead to tell them I am on my way.

"If they hurt Hali, if any of you do, I'm going to murder you all. One by one, and that's a damn promise," I tell them. I try to keep my voice calm, unlike my emotions, as I rest back in the seat.

"I don't doubt it. We all know who you are," the man driving the car says, his purple eyes catching mine in the mirror. His cloak hood falls down, showing off his rugged, strong-looking face, a five o'clock shadow, and a seriousness to his tight-lipped expression. The grumpy Protector looks like he has a stick up his ass.

"What are you waiting for? Drive, grumpy," I smirk, keeping my emotions hidden because I have no idea where they are taking me or what they want. Whatever it is, I'm never helping them. I'd rather kill them first.

Chapter Five

EVIE

"WELCOME TO THE ISLAND OF THE PROTECTORS and the royal court," grumpy says in the most unwelcoming tone ever, as we drive straight towards an empty looking cliff. Finally, one of them talks to me. I know the Protector in the passenger seat is Connor, only because he spoke to Grumpy once. It's been a dead quiet three-hour drive, and I'm starving. I also have no plan to escape, and no idea where we even are. I look over at Grumpy, and then at the speed he is driving as I think about what he just said. I look behind us at the car following us, the one I know Hali is in and then back to the cliff. *Is he really going to drive us off a cliff?*

"Are you fucking crazy? Don't drive off a cliff–" I stop shouting when the car goes off the cliff, but it's not a cliff at all, it's a long road that just appears out of nowhere. *A gold freakin road*. I lean forward, looking at the five gold towers in the distance and the many gold roads that stretched across the sea leading up to the little city. It's a hidden city, one I've heard of, but from no one that actually had any proof of its existence. Just rumours on the streets. Rumours from demons that say they have been here, but you can never trust a word from a demon. *If anyone knows that, it's me.*

"So, I take it you guys like gold then?" I ask sarcastically. There is a crap-ton of gold stuff. Any thief would have a field day here.

"Do you like blue?" Connor asks pointedly, smirking as he puts his hood down, and I finally can see some of his handsome features. He has golden hair, wavy and messy, but out of the way of his gold eyes. He reminds me of a lion in an attractive way. I don't answer him, knowing he is just taking the piss out of my blue hair.

"Blue, are you not going to reply?" Connor asks me, and the other Protector whacks him on the arm before returning his hand to the wheel.

"Don't flirt with her, idiot! She is a fucking assassin," he snaps at Connor.

"Trex, don't be so stuck up. They are going to

kill her anyway, if she doesn't help us, why not be nice?" Connor says, his voice downright seductive. He reminds me of succubus demons; they have sexy voices that can make you do anything they ask.

"You mean why not try to fuck her *before* they kill her?" Trex replies.

"I'm right here," I interrupt, and then slowly drift my eyes up and down Connor's muscular form. "Although I don't mind the fucking idea, but that might have to wait." Connor smirks, opening his pretty mouth to say something, but Trex interrupts.

"Both of you, shut it. Connor, do remember you have a job to do, and you can't afford to fuck this one up. None of us can," Trex's harsh words do something to Connor, as he sits back and does just as he is told. I don't bother speaking to either of them anymore, looking around at the secret damn city as we drive up to the towers. When we get closer, I notice they are less like towers and more like city high-rises. All glass windows on one side, and gold walls on the others. The Protectors drive us straight towards the biggest tower in the middle, and I focus on the outside. There are no Protectors to be seen anywhere. It's like a ghost town in here. Holy shit, the sidewalk is even gold. *Where the hell do they get the money for a place like this?* I glance up at the two angel statues outside the building, one on each side. Humans say Protectors have a tiny amount of both angel and demon blood, making them perfect to protect them from both.

"Where are all your people? Children?" I ask, distracting myself from my thoughts. This is a place I never thought I'd ever be.

"They know you are coming here, so they have all hidden," Trex answers me.

"That's a little bit of an overreaction, don't you think?" I ask, trying not to laugh at the serious look he gives me through the mirror.

"No, it's no overreaction at all. Now shut up," he snaps, and this time, I do laugh as I sit back. After about ten minutes of driving through the town, we pull up to the largest building. I look behind us, not seeing the car Hali was in. *I can't believe I let myself get so distracted.*

"Where is Hali?" I demand.

"She will be taken to a private room and kept safe. Only those with Protector's blood can enter most of the buildings here. They have wards," Connor warns me, and I have to bite my lip to stop myself from saying anything stupid. Connor locks eyes with me, only for a second.

"She won't be harmed. *We* are not the monsters here," he promises me, almost sounding honest enough for me to believe him. *Almost.*

"She is a child, and your people just held a dagger to her throat," I bite out.

"You know as well as I what she is, what she will be. She will be a monster, and you won't be able to stop her. A witch's mark is their destiny, and what she will do, will get her and everyone near her killed," Connor retorts.

"Hali is no monster, nor will she ever be. You and your stuck-up race judge everyone before even giving them a chance," I say, giving him a disgusted look.

"You say 'your race', like you aren't one of us," Trex interrupts, and I shake my head, not bothering with the annoying Protectors any more. I try to open my door the moment the car stops, but it's locked and gets me damn annoyed enough to want to break one of the windows.

"Child locks," Connor says, a smirk on his lips before he gets out of the car at the same time Trex does. I'm forced to wait for Trex and Connor to speak to three Protectors in hoods outside the car, and not able to hear what they say. I roll my eyes and climb over the middle part of the seat, letting myself out Trex's door. They don't notice me until I slam the door shut and lean against it. They all turn to face me with shocked looks. *Did they really think I'd just sit there?* The other three Protectors actually take a step back, their hands going to their swords on their hips beneath their cloaks.

"Are we going inside, or what? I'm getting bored, and I want to know what the fuck you all want with me," I ask, making Connor cough on a laugh, and Trex narrow his eyes at me.

"Stand down, she won't attack us," Trex says and waves his hand at the glass doors of the building. "After you miss–"

"My name is Evie, none of that 'miss' crap," I say, pushing myself off the car and walking towards the doors. I pass the three Protectors, and I can't help myself.

"Boo," I whisper, and one jumps back, falling onto his butt. I laugh as I walk away and head into the building as the automatic doors open.

Chapter Six

EVIE

"Nice place, all shiny and shit. Not that I expected anything different," I drawl, lifting my head, looking around at the very gold and shiny building. There are five elevators in the middle, made of glass, and they stretch all the way up to the top of the building. At the top, the ceiling is made of gold, but all the glass in here makes it seem bright. There is no one at the circular counter in the middle of the room, which strikes me as odd. Three Protectors, in perfect and expensive-looking suits come out of one of the elevators, and they stop dead in their tracks. They all panic, hurrying back in the elevator, and one keeps pressing the button again and again until the door shuts.

"We don't need any of your comments on the

decor," Trex snaps, glaring at the scared Protectors in the elevator as it goes up. He walks ahead, and I try not to laugh at his stuck-up attitude. I follow him to the middle elevator, getting in with him and Connor. We are silent as Trex presses the button for the twelfth floor. The other Protectors wait by the door, their hands on their swords as they watch.

"Out of interest, why am I here? What could you possibly want from me?" I ask them, wondering if I can get them to tell me. I don't like the unknown, and this whole situation is exactly that.

"We need your help," Connor says, and Trex grabs his arm.

"Don't say another word," he growls out, and Connor jerks his arm away, keeping his eyes locked on Trex. Why would they need my help? I wrack my brain trying to think of anything the Protectors could want from me, but I don't come up with anything. It doesn't make any sense. I look back at the guys, and see them both still glaring at each other as they seem to have a silent conversation.

"There is a lot of tension here, is it sexual? I could totally see that happening between the two of you," I ask innocently, and Connor chokes on a laugh as Trex's face goes red.

"It's best you shut up now, blue," Connor says,

still laughing a little bit. We all go silent as the elevator door opens to a long corridor. This corridor is lit with white spotlights on the floor, that make a path to massive glass doors at the end. The glass is coloured with red swords in a circle, and a woman on her knees. The woman has runes down her arms, each one is the colour they light up when you use them. The blue for holy fire, which burns demons, and it looks like a rose. The red rune for portals, which looks like an archway in a circle. The white rune, which is shaped like a sword in a triangle and lets us heal, and finally the last rune. The black rune shaped like a skull. The black rune is one I've never used before, and I don't have a clue what it does. I have a feeling like I shouldn't use it, and I usually listen to those kinds of feelings. *Well, most of the time.*

"A little advice, be respectful," Connor suggests as we get to the door.

"Sorry, that's *really* not a part of my plan," I smile innocently as the doors are opened. Connor and Trex walk slightly in front of me, blocking my view of the room, but they did just what I wanted them to do. I quickly slide my dagger out of the holder on my hip and jump on Connor's back, holding the dagger against his neck.

"Fuck," Connor mutters, holding his hands in the air.

"Don't move. You wouldn't want me to slip," I say sweetly next to his ear, holding the dagger close. The room is dead silent as I look around, ignoring Trex as he glares at me. There are three thrones in the center of the room, and the floor is made of red glass by the looks of it. I glance around at the five gold statues in the room; four of them are men, and there is one woman. She has long hair, and a smile on her face as she reaches up in the air for something, and for some reason, she looks familiar to me. She has runes etched on her face and a crown right in the middle. It makes me freeze, but not enough to forget where I am. I pull my eyes away from the statue to the four hooded people in the room.

"Kill him if you must," the man in the middle says, pulling his hood down. The man has dark skin, brown eyes, and his hair is shaved off, so I can see the tattoos on his head. They look like symbols, maybe even runes, but I'm not close enough to see. He has a flame symbol on his forehead, and when the other three men lower their hoods, I see they all wear the symbol. It's still clear to me who the leader is as they let him speak.

"Let me go. They won't care if you kill me. You

should have held the dagger to Trex's throat if you wanted a useful hostage," Connor bites out. I look over at Trex, who watches me carefully. I know he is waiting for a chance to attack me. I grin, moving my dagger away as I jump off Connor's back and hold my hands up. They aren't going to attack me. I can see it in the way they stand. Everything points to Connor telling me the truth earlier, they need me for something, and I might as well find out what. Connor steps away from me, rubbing his neck.

"Okay, okay. I'll play nice. So, what do you want?" I turn away from looking at Connor to ask the men who are obviously in charge.

"My name is Keeper Cadean, and quite simply, we need your help," he tells me with a dead serious expression.

"Why would I help your kind? You've hardly welcomed me with open arms," I say, with a sarcastic laugh, and he nods in agreement.

"We will never welcome you into the Protectors, because of our knowledge of who you are. We still must make a deal with you for your help," he states, folding his hands together.

"And who, exactly, am I?" I ask, wanting to know what they think.

"A killer, an assassin, and a thief. You could

never be trusted in the royal Protector's city," he states simply.

"Explain what you want, I'm getting bored with all this," I say, waving my hand.

"Two nights ago, our three princesses were taken. Our princesses were five days away from a ceremony that would have made one of them our queen, and we have no other royal heirs," Cadean says tightly.

"Do you think I took them? Are you kidding?" I say, with wide eyes, trying not to laugh.

"No, we do not think you took them. The princesses are the most powerful of our kind. They would not be taken by a simple assassin," Trex laughs condescendingly, and I narrow my eyes at him.

"I could have, if I had known they existed that is," I mutter.

"Our royal family is the best kept secret of the Protectors," Trex tells me.

"Then why haven't you gone after them yourselves? You all have runes like me," I say.

"On the same night, our runes' powers were stolen. We believe the kidnapper placed demon power into our water supply and food somehow. We won't be able to use our rune powers until it is out of our system, which will be around two weeks," Connor explains to me.

"Right, so let me get this straight. Your princesses have been taken, you have no powers, and you want me to *what*, exactly?" I ask.

"We have information that suggests the princesses are on the bottom level of Hell. We believe a couple of overlord demons took them for their power. We want you to rescue them," Cadean says, and all I can do is laugh. *They have to be kidding.*

"I told you she wouldn't help us. She only helps herself," Trex snaps, giving me a disgusted look, and I have to resist the urge to stick my tongue out at the moody fucker.

"We have something Evie wants, and for that, she will help us," Cadean states plainly, his voice confident enough to make me pause and look back at him. He stands still, his brown eyes watching me carefully, like he knows I'm close to flipping out and escaping this hell hole of shiny crap.

"Like what?" I ask.

"I know why you are hunted, and I know what your rune name is. I can tell you about your past, more about who you are, and I can make sure you are never hunted again. You help us, and you will have all the answers you have been searching for, and you won't have to hide anymore," he tells me, and I pause for a second, running his bargain over in my mind. I don't know anything about my life, and he could tell me everything. I know my parents had to be Protectors, it's the only way I could have my marks.

"And you will let Hali walk free, pretending you never saw her?" I ask, because she has to come with the deal.

"We will never speak of the death-marked witch, nor tell her kind she is alive," Cadean nods. I slide my dagger back into the holder and cross my arms.

"Getting into Hell is no problem, but surviving there is no easy task. I've only been to the top layer, but I do know the two layers below it are impossible to survive alone. I will need some of your people to come with me. Preferably ones you don't mind losing if they die," I say, and Cadean nods his head at Trex.

"I will travel with you. Connor and my brother, Nix, will join us," he says firmly. I nod, looking back to Cadean.

"I will take Hali and leave to prepare," I say.

"The witch stays here until you return. Think of her as a symbol of trust between us. After all, you are the legendary assassin who cannot be trusted," Cadean tells me.

"I want to see her before I leave then," I demand, and Cadean nods. I turn and walk towards the door with Connor and Trex following. I stop, letting them open the door and look once more back at Cadean.

"I always keep my word, and you'd best keep yours. If anything happens to her, there will be nothing between every powerless Protector and me. Keep that in mind. Plus, I'm sure the demons would *love* to know that demon power stops rune powers," I say, my voice pitched low and with a smile laced with malice. He nods his head, almost in a bow, yet keeping his eyes locked onto mine. I don't need to hear his response as I walk out of the room because I saw the fear flash in his eyes, and that's all I need to know. They will keep their side of the deal.

Chapter Seven.

EVIE

"Evie!" Hali shouts as she runs over to me, nearly knocking me to the floor as she hugs me. I pull away, looking her over and making sure there isn't anything out of place or wrong with her before taking a deep breath. Even if they did promise not to hurt her, I still wouldn't believe it until I had seen her for myself.

"Are you okay?" I ask, and she nods, her eyes flashing to Connor and Trex who have followed me into the room. She looks scared, and I don't blame her. They are a little intimidating, especially to someone like Hali who hasn't been around Protectors before. Or you know, giant men in cloaks with swords. She only knows I kill Protectors like them sometimes, and that I think they are bad people.

"Ignore them, they are stalking me now, and I can't get rid of them for a bit. Just try to think of them as big teddy bears or something," I say, making her chuckle and Trex growl something under his breath. I whistle as I look around at the room they have Hali in for the first time. Everything is white and black, spotless and expensive. The room we are in is a multi-functional room, with a small kitchen, a lounge area, and a double bed near the windows that overlook the city. Everything looks top of the range.

"At least you have a nice room for a bit," I say, and she widens her eyes.

"You're not taking me home? I have to stay here?" she questions with a slight tremor in her voice. I walk over to the sofa, encouraging her to sit next to me. She does, watching me with those pale eyes that seem to know what I'm thinking before I've said it. I keep my voice low, even though I'm sure Trex and Connor can hear me.

"I have to do something for the Protectors, and it's dangerous. I'm not going to lie to you and say I will certainly be back here in a few weeks, but I promise I will do everything I can to get back to you," I promise her, hating when tears begin to stream down her face.

"I don't want you to go," she says, shaking her head and leaning over to wrap her arms around me. I hold her for only a few seconds, before pulling back enough that I can whisper in her ear.

"I will send someone to save you. Even if it's not me, if for whatever reason I can't make it back, I *will* make sure you will be safe. Do not worry," I tell her because I have friends, okay demons, that will do anything for money. Including breaking in here and saving Hali.

"Don't go," she begs, holding onto me tightly.

"Be safe and do as they ask, alright?" I ask, and she wipes some tears away as she lets go of my hand. "You're my family, and you're stronger than this. We might not share blood, but we share a spirit. I know it's in there somewhere." She glances away, before looking back and giving me a determined expression.

"Yes."

"That's my girl," I grin, trying to keep my worry at bay as I stand up and walk to the door. I look back at her once, seeing her sitting on the sofa, and her expression hasn't changed. She can do this, I can see it, and I will be back for her.

"I'll see you soon," I tell her, knowing I'm going to do anything I need to, so that I can get back here.

To her. Connor opens the door, sympathy flashing in his eyes for a second as I look at him before I walk past. I don't need or want his sympathy. He was one of the people that helped capture and kidnap Hali.

"We have a car ready, but we need to make a plan," Trex comments as we walk towards the elevator we came up in.

"I have a plan," I state, and he raises a perfect black bushy eyebrow at me.

"Do you care to enlighten us with it?" he asks sarcastically. I wait until we are all standing in the elevator before I answer him.

"Have you ever been to Hell? Do you know anything of what you have ahead of you?" I ask them.

"No, I've never been personally, but I've heard—" I cut him off.

"Then you haven't got a clue what we will need to survive there. We will need a demon's protection to get through without being killed, and I know a demon who owes me a favour," I say.

"We don't work with demons," Trex huffs.

"You do now," I say, walking out of the elevator when it gets to the bottom. This building is just as empty as the council one. It's all glass again, and gold walls with crystal chandeliers. There are dozens of doors, which must be rooms for the other Protectors, but we only see one or two around, and they quickly run away.

"In Hell, the first layer is freezing cold. You will need to wrap up warm and bring plenty of weapons considering you're powerless."

"We will do that, but what about the second and third layer? We heard it's different," Connor inquires, but I don't have a clue, and the only demon that would know, is no one I'm going to ask.

"Not a clue, but it is likely as bad as you are thinking it is," I say dryly. It's not a place I'm looking forward to going. My first and only trip to Hell when I was eighteen was bad enough.

"Do you have a phone?" I ask them both as we stop outside the building. Connor pulls his phone out of his pocket, unlocking it, and handing it to me. I quickly type an address with my number underneath it in his notes, before handing it back before handing it back.

"Be there at eight tonight. Dress in something a human or demon would wear to a nightclub. No suits or cloaks," I say, looking down at their outfits on purpose.

"We must leave for Hell, not go to wherever this is," Trex growls.

"This is our only chance. You asked for my help, so you're going to have to trust me," I say, going to walk away when Trex grabs my arm, pulling me to him. I look up as his green eyes stare down at me in anger and distrust.

"If you betray us, I *will* kill you. I don't need my runes to do that, do you understand me, Evie?" he asks, using my name for the first time, and I grin, pushing my body closer to his.

"Totally. By the way, I've always liked a demanding guy. They are always best in bed," I say, flirting with him to annoy him. As predicted, he pushes me away, scowling at me. I laugh, walking to the car, and look back at them.

"See you later, boys." I finger wave with a slight smirk.

Chapter Eight

CONNOR

"SHE WAS NOT WHAT I EXPECTED. NOT AT ALL," Trex says as we watch the car taking Evie away, not looking away once. I think he expects her to jump out and start attacking us, or something. Until today, until I met her, that's what I'd have expected her to do as well. She is nothing like I anticipated. Shiny, soft-looking blue hair that falls in waves around her. Glowing, fiery blue eyes and a killer body. If I'd met her under any other circumstances, I would do anything to get into her knickers.

"What do you think the keepers know about her?" I ask him, because I didn't know they knew anything. No one knows anything of her. She is just a rumour, an outcast who kills anyone that goes near her, indiscriminately. *But that's a lie.* The witch she protects is proof she doesn't kill everyone. She held a dagger to my throat today, and if she didn't care about killing, she would have killed me.

"Something she is willing to fight to find out," Trex says, just as Evie's car disappears through the barrier.

"We should go and get your brother," I state, wishing Trex hadn't suggested bringing him on this mission. He is the last person you want to take into Hell with you.

"Yeah, he might need sobering up before tonight," Trex replies, turning and walking down the street. We get to the first building across, and rather than going into it, we walk around it to the back entrance. It's hidden, but nearly every Protector knows it's here. The smell of smoke and alcohol hits me when we walk through the door, and I pull it shut behind us both.

"Let's split up to look for him," Trex suggests, knowing this place is underground and about five layers. It takes a lot to get us drunk or stoned, and this is the only place for Protectors to safely come and let off some steam.

"Sure," I comment, walking to the left, and he goes right. I walk down the glass-walled hall ways, looking at the sofas and bars, not seeing Nix anywhere. I nearly to the end of the corridor when I spot him. He is sitting on a sofa, two girls at his side in dresses that leave little to the imagination. He has a bottle of vodka in his hand as he looks up at the ceiling and blows out smoke. Nix doesn't have a shirt on, showing off his chest and arms that are completely covered in tattoos. His black curly hair falls all over the place as he hasn't bothered having it cut in a while, and by the looks of him, I bet he has been in here for a few days doing fuck knows what. *Great, he is seriously fucked.* I open the glass door, walking straight over and standing in front of him. He doesn't even notice as the girl on his right starts climbing on his lap and kissing his neck.

"Nix," I shout, kicking his leg, making him nearly drop his bottle as he jumps and shoots his head forward. I look at the girls, vaguely recognising them.

"You two disappear, or I'll tell your families you're in here," I say, keeping an eye on Nix's annoyed face as the two girls jump up off the sofa and practically run out of the room.

"Buzz kill, Con. We could have shared," he grins.

"Maybe another time. We have shit to do, and

you need to be sober," I tell him, and he groans, lifting his bottle and downing it. I reach over, snatching it from him and smashing it on the floor.

"I'm not fucking around, Nix, now get your shit together," I tell him, just as Trex gets to my side.

"Do I have to knock you out and carry your ass out of here like last week?" he says, crossing his arms.

"No, I can fucking walk," he mutters, glaring at his brother and stands up, swaying a little before promptly passing out, his body smacking onto the floor.

"I'll get him," I sigh, patting Trex's shoulder. He glares at his brother and putsg his hand on my chest to stop me.

"She wouldn't want this. We both lost her, and *this* is not how she would want anyone to react," he points at his brother. "Our sister didn't die saving his ass, so he could drink his life away. I will deal with him," he says, leaning down and picking up his brother over his shoulder. I feel sorry for Trex and Nix. They lost both of their parents, and more recently, their sister. Nix drinks the memories away, and Trex, well, he pretends nothing happened.

"Meet you outside at seven tonight," Trex says,

and carries his brother out of the room. I walk over to the bar, paying Nix's bill before leaving. I just pray Trex can get Nix in any state to be of use to us tonight.

Chapter Nine

NIX

"I'M NOT GOING TO HELL TO SAVE ANYONE! YOU'RE fucking kidding, right?" I exclaim, sitting up on my bed. From my seat, I can see my brother's disappointed glare levied in my direction. The door bangs open, and Connor walks in, handing me a glass of water. I glance around at my apartment; the bed, the sofa, and the small kitchen are all that are in it, other than one other door that leads to a bathroom. It's empty other than the discarded take away boxes and drained liquor bottles littered around. I don't even remember how I got back here last night.

"I'd prefer vodka," I say, taking the drink, and holding a hand to my head as the room spins.

"Yeah well, tough shit. We need you," Connor replies dryly, leaning against the wall.

"Why me, again?" I question, and Trex groans as he narrows his eyes at me.

"Didn't you tell him?" Connor asks.

"I just barely woke him up, and I think he only heard the bit about going into Hell," Trex responds, and I lean back on my pillows and look at them both.

"The princesses have been stolen, and we need to go to Hell to get them back," Connor says, like it's a normal thing to wake someone up and inform them of.

"I'm sorry they are gone, but who took them? How do we know they are in Hell?" I ask the important questions.

"The keepers won't tell us how they know, and they don't have a clue who took them, apparently," Connor replies.

"Right, so we can go and die for them, but they won't tell us shit?" I ask, a hollow laugh following my words as Connor and Trex don't reply. There's a knock on the door, which breaks up the awkward silence, and Connor opens the door. A keeper is standing still outside the door, his hood covering his face, so I can't see who it is.

"May I enter?" the keeper asks, and Connor holds the door open for him, letting him in. The unfamiliar keeper lowers his hood, looking around at my apartment with clear disgust before speaking.

"What I tell you now is a secret, and many of the keepers would have me killed just for telling you," he says, and I look him over. The keeper is old, one of the oldest I bet, with white roots and brown hair, but I honestly don't care. I don't have anything to do with keepers or any of their crap since they let my sister die. Connor shuts the door before walking over, and sitting on my sofa as I get out of the bed and go to my kitchen. I open the doors, seeing the cabinet I usually store my alcohol in is empty, and I spot the empty bottles next to the sink. I turn and glare at my brother, who just grins. *Asshole.*

"Who are you?" I turn and ask the keeper, wanting his name before I kick him, my brother, and Connor out of my apartment.

"Keeper Grey," he says simply.

"Well, Keeper Grey, nice to meet you, but you need to leave, and take these assholes with you while you're at it," I say, and he shakes his head.

"I cannot do that. You need my advice and my help."

"I don't need fuck from you," I snarl. Connor narrows his eyes at me, sharply shaking his head.

"And don't start with the lecture I can see you're about to launch into, Trex," I warn, not even needing to look at him to know he is about to start off on one.

"Fine. I will speak to Trex and Connor, and you may listen if you wish," Keeper Grey says, moving to sit on the sofa next to Connor.

"The princesses were not kidnapped, they just went missing. We assumed a kidnapping, instead of considering the alternative of the likelihood that they walked out of here," he says, and there's a tense silence. I know the princesses well enough to know that wouldn't have happened. They are pampered here; they can do whatever they like, and one of them was about to be crowned queen. *Who in their right mind would just walk away from that?*

"The princesses wouldn't have just deserted the throne, not all of them," Trex points out.

"They did. Or they left. There was no forced entry. Of that, I am certain," Keeper Grey informs us.

"Then why do the keepers think the princesses are in Hell?" Trex asks.

"We had no choice but to search the princesses'

rooms, and in one, we found something that only an overlord demon could have. A token of an overlord's sin. They always keep their sin close to them, and never show or tell anyone unless they are family or very close," he explains, and I watch Trex tighten his fists in anger and sharply look away.

"The princesses are close to a demon overlord? How is that possible?" Connor exclaims in clear shock. Demon overlords are not our friends. We hunt them—not let them anywhere near our royals. *Our most protected.*

"I am as clueless as you. I simply could not let you go into Hell without knowing all of the truth, or the simple fact that they might not actually be there," he says, standing up. "I wouldn't tell the assassin about this. If she knew, she wouldn't take you to Hell, and while we are powerless, we need her."

"What do you know about the assassin? Who is she? Who are her parents?" I ask, and he looks towards me. I watch his expression carefully, and see many emotions flash in his eyes as he tries to decide what to tell me. I'm not the best at judging people's reactions, but I have a feeling this assassin means something to him.

"I know everything there is know about her, but

I am bound to never to speak a word. I promised her father I would keep her secret and protect her. That is why I am telling you all I know, because you will be protecting her, in a way, on your travels," he says.

"Who is her father?" I ask.

"I cannot say," he replies, almost sadly, and lifts his hood, walking to the door and opening it up. "Good luck, Protectors."

"That was . . . weird," Connor says as Keeper Grey shuts the door after himself.

"I'm coming with you," I tell them firmly.

"Why have you changed your mind?" Trex asks, genuinely surprised, if his voice is anything to go by.

"To keep you fuckers alive, that's why. You will need me," I say, and both Connor and Trex laugh.

"If that's what you need to tell yourself, fine," Trex says walking away, opening the door and looking back over his shoulder. "But take a damn shower, you stink, brother."

I laugh, walking into my bathroom as Connor leaves, to do just that.

Chapter Ten

EVIE

"Do you have food?" I ask the man, who pushes me away, and I fall to the ground. The demon doesn't even look back as he walks away. I look down, bursting into tears as rain pours down on me, and I sink further into the mud. My fifth birthday was two days ago, and it was also the last time that I had eaten. My parents had yelled as I accidently set their rug on fire. They said I wasn't human, that I was unnatural, and I had to leave. I screamed and screamed for them to not leave me, but they did.

"Hey, are you okay?" a woman asks, running over and picking me up off the floor. She holds me close, folding her cloak around me as I cry, and she rubs my back. The woman waves her hand, a blue light covering her hand, and I hear a door open. The woman carries me into the warm room,

putting me down on something soft, but I'm too scared to open my eyes.

"Hunny, you are safe now," she says soothingly.

"I'm alone now," I whimper.

"No, not anymore," the woman says. I open my eyes, seeing a dark-skinned woman kneeling in front of me. She has long black hair, a weird mark on her right cheek, and a big smile. She has on a long dress, big grey eyes, and I don't think she is a demon. I don't know what she is, but she seems nice.

"I'm scared."

"I know, but if you will trust me, I won't leave you alone. The world isn't good all the time, but I think if you can do one good thing, it's a step in the right direction," she says and stands up. "Do you like hot chocolate? I have some I can make you, and then we'll get you a meal."

"Yes, please," I whisper, and she smiles before walking away. I was never alone from that day on, even when I thought I always would be.

"Here, stop here," I say to the taxi driver after a street light flashes in my eyes, and snaps me out the horrible memory. My human adoptive parents left me here on my fifth birthday and never looked back. I guess I was lucky they thought I was a demon, even though the blue hair should have tipped them off, and they left me here, where the Protectors couldn't find me. The taxi driver instantly puts the breaks on and stops the taxi. He gives me a questioning look at where we've stopped. It looks like an empty field, but only supes would be able to see what it really is. I pay him, get out of the taxi, and watch as he turns around and drives off. I smooth down my tight, red dress, hoping that the dagger on my thighs can't be seen. *I hate dresses.* The wind pushes my hair in my face and reminds me that I left my hair down, so it covers up the knife attached to my back. One bonus for having waist-length hair. Weapons aren't really allowed here, but everyone brings them. It's too dangerous not to. I have to wait ten more minutes for the Protectors' car to show up. Connor gets out first, shocking me a little to see him looking normal. And hot. Very fucking hot. His blonde hair is styled to the left, and he has on black trousers paired with a loose blue shirt that has a few buttons undone. I can't see any weapons on him, but I'm not stupid enough to think he hasn't hidden them somewhere.

"Wow," Connor whistles as he looks me up and down, but my attention strays to the stranger that gets out of the back seat. He has messy black hair and a white shirt that is undone except for two buttons at the bottom, so I can see all the black ink covering his chest. It stops just before his neck. I lift my eyes to his green ones, that remind me of Trex. This must be the brother whose name I can't remember.

"You didn't tell me she was fucking gorgeous, Con," the brother muses, eyeing me up like a snack. The door slams shut, just as Trex walks over.

"That's because she is working with us, Nix, not here to fuck us," Trex says, making me laugh, and his eyes narrow on mine.

"What is so funny?" he asks as I roll my eyes at his tight, dark-green shirt—the way every button is done up—and his black trousers. He still looks too formal, but it will have to do.

"Your denial that you want me. I can see it," I grin, and he scowls at me. "Anyway, boys, try to keep your mouths shut in here. Demons aren't really fans of Protectors."

"It is our job to keep them in line, so I'd expect not," Trex replies dryly.

"Keep in line, yes. But you guys send them to hell so often for just *living*, they hate you," I tell them honestly. Most of the time, the demons are unfairly accused, and there is no trial to find out what happened. They are just sent back to hell without questioning, or killed. Most of the time they are killed. I turn around, walking to the small gate and pushing the wooden revolving gate which lets us through the barrier.

"Fucking hell," I hear Nix curse behind me as the field disappears, and the demon underground appears. There are metal containers piled everywhere, the ones at the bottom are open with shops inside and the market in front of them. Other containers lead into diners, clubs, and other rooms. Music blasts from a nearby speaker, and people walk past us like we aren't even here, dressed in similar clothes or cloaks. All sorts of people live here, but the demons run it. Mainly overlord demons who are meant to be banned from Earth. *Let's hope the Protectors don't see any of those around.* There are five demon undergrounds as far as I know. I should know because I grew up in them. When you are hunted by Protectors like demons are, then demons become your friends and allies.

"Not a word about this place," I warn them, though I know it's likely they are going to die in Hell, anyway, and never get a chance to tell anyone, so I'm not too worried. I only want to get my ass back out of hell with the princesses, not them. "This way." I nod my head to the left and walk down the stone pathway. I keep my eyes down as I pass several people, not wanting anyone to know I'm here with these Protectors. I know too many people here, and so many wouldn't take it well to see me walking Protectors into their homes. Hopefully, no one will notice they are something more than human. We finally get to the building I want. It's the only one around here that is made from bricks and concrete. It used to be a school, I think, but it's been changed and now houses a nightclub for the most dangerous demons.

"Don't drink or eat anything in here that I don't give you, trust me," I stop to warn them before walking up to the entrance. Two demon bouncers are outside, and one holds his arm in front of me to stop me. I can't see their faces, only their cloaks and their red skin, letting me know they are likely very powerful demons.

"Password," the one who stopped me asks.

"Sempiternum daemonum futurum oriri," I say quietly, and he lowers his hand, letting me in with a glance. Connor walks closer to my side as we walk in the house, and down the long corridor that leads to the club.

"What did that mean? And how do you speak Latin?" Connor asks curiously.

"All demons speak Latin, some more so than English, and I grew up with demons. Do you not bother speaking to them before you kill them?" I ask him, and he doesn't reply. "I said 'demons will rise' in Latin, because the people here believe it."

"You think of demons as people," he says as he figures out my feelings on demons. They *are* people. They have feelings; they fall in love, and they protect their families. Demons are better than humans in my experience. The only demons that I don't think of as people are overlords, and we are heading to see one. Overlords are said to be thousands of years old, but I don't know if that's true. I doubt it, it's likely just a rumour.

"That's one of the biggest mistakes of your kind, that you don't see them as people," I sneer at him and walk faster so that I'm ahead of him. I push the wooden doors open at the end of the corridor and walk into the night club. The loud, thumping music immediately assaults my ears. I look around, seeing demon women dancing with human men on the dance floor. They are succubus demons by the looks of their blue skin, black hair, and tantalizing bodies as they seduce the human men in suits out of their money. A female waitress, a lower-class demon with red skin and black eyes stops in front of us, offering us a drink from the tray she is holding.

"No, thanks. Do you speak English?" I ask her, and she pauses, giving me a worried nod.

"Good. I'm looking for Seth," I ask, and her eyes widen. She moves to run away, and I grab her arm, stopping her.

"Tell Seth that Evie is here. He will want to see me," I explain to her and let her go, watching as she runs away.

"Seems not just Protectors run from you," Trex sarcastically comments. *Asshole.*

"She will tell him I'm here. Seth usually has company, so we will have to wait," I reply calmly, not rising to Trex's taunts.

"I think it's time for a drink, and time we got to know each other better. We are going to Hell after all, we should at least know a few things about each other," Nix says, walking to the bar without asking for my permission. *I think I like him, he seems like an asshole.* I follow him over, stopping him when he lifts a hand to order.

"Let me order, unless you want to wake up in a demon's bed with your soul missing," I say, lifting my own hand, and the demon bartender runs over.

The bartender is young, with big blue eyes and a tired expression.

"Four normals, Jack Daniels if you have it. In fact, leave the bottle," I tell him, and the bartender stares at me for a second before running off.

"Has that happened to you?" Connor asks with wide eyes as he waits at my side for the bartender to get our drinks. I walk over to an empty booth with a table, sliding into a seat. The guys sit next to me, Connor on my left and Nix on my right. As suspected, Trex sits as far away from me as possible.

"Not personally, but I know someone it did happen to. He died the next day; it was a shame. I liked him," I say with a grin that seems to worry them all. Luckily for them, the bartender comes over with four shot glasses and a bottle of Jack Daniels.

"I've opened a tab, pay later, assassin," the bartender says, bowing low and walking away. I reach for the bottle, but Nix is quicker, grinning at me as he opens it.

"Too slow, love," he says.

"Not another nickname. It's bad enough what he calls me," I point a finger at Connor, who leans closer, picking up a strand of my blue hair, twirling it around.

"But, *Blue*, it suits you," he says seductively. Then he asks in a more serious tone, "How did you get your hair like this? Is it dyed?" I pick up the drink Nix poured for me, downing it before answering him. I'm tempted to lie, but there really isn't much point. These guys won't survive long, anyway.

"I've always had blue hair. I had a witch friend, who said the only way to get my hair this colour was to use the blue rune when I was too young, and for far too long. I must have been almost killed as a baby or something, and I called my rune subconsciously," I tell them, and Trex stares at me as he downs his shot, pouring himself another one. I feel them all staring, but I just hold my hand out for the bottle, waiting until Trex hands it to me. I don't bother with the glass, just drinking straight from the bottle and slamming it back on the table, loving the burn of the liquor down my throat.

"I've heard of a Protector who has had white hair most of his life. He used the white rune when he was four years old to heal himself from a deadly attack, and it turned his hair white and he couldn't change it," Trex says, and for a moment, we stare at each other. For a moment, I think he might be redeemable, and not a total asshole, but then he keeps talking. "It's likely your parents knew what you were and tried to kill you for it."

"The blue rune is holy fire. Holy fire only kills demons, so I wouldn't have called it to kill my parents or protect myself from them. It's *more* likely demons tried to kill me and my parents, and I survived somehow," I tell them, and a deep voice clears his throat from the end of the table.

"You called for me, Evie darling?"

Chapter Eleven

EVIE

I LOOK OVER TO THE DEMON OVERLORD LEANING against the table, a smirk on his pretty lips as he watches me. Seth has always been pretty, but his pretty face doesn't work on me, though he has tried many, many times. I know how much of a shithead he can be, and I don't sleep with assholes like him. He has white hair, braided at his neck, and dark-red eyes that reveal how smart he is, but hidden from most by their beauty. He is the very definition of deadly beauty, just like his brothers, I've met, are. His suit shirt is loose, and there are lipstick stains on his neck telling me he had been having a good night until I interrupted. He smirks, looking around at the Protectors, and then back to me.

"Interesting friends you've got here, Evie darling," he drawls.

"We need to speak. Privately," I answer, watching as he stands taller, and nods his head to the left.

"My room then," he says. Connor gets out of the booth, and I follow, looking back to see Trex pull the bottle of Jack out of Nix's grip, and glare at him. *Clearly, there are some problems in paradise.* We walk through the nightclub to a small set of stairs where two demons stand guard. They glance at Seth, who simply nods, and they let us all past. At the top of the stairs, Seth opens the door to a large room. It has a glass floor, so we can see the people dancing on the dance floor below. Trex closes the door behind us, and I wait as Seth goes over to a little table, pouring himself a drink.

"Do you want one?" he asks.

"No," I answer for us all.

"So, Evie darling, are you going to explain why the *fuck* you have brought three Protectors into my home?" he asks, his eyes starting to glow from his anger.

"It's complicated, but I'm not here to talk about them. You owe me a favour, and I need to collect," I say, and he chokes on his drink.

"You're kidding me? Right?"

"No, not one bit," I bite out.

"What do you want exactly?" he enquires.

"I need to get to the bottom layer of Hell, and for that, I need an overlord demon at my side," I say, and he laughs, until he meets my eyes and realises how serious I am.

"Fuck, Evie darling, that's a death sentence, even for me," he says and pulls his phone out.

"I know someone who might go with you, but I can't," he says, and I swear under my breath. If I can't get an overlord to come with me, I'll have to fight to get into the third layer. No one is that strong, or that stupid.

"I saved your child, does that not earn me a debt?" I say. Three years ago, his five-year old-daughter was kidnapped, and everyone was called to search. I was the one that found her and brought her back alive when no one else could have.

"And I helped you by not warning every demon here that you walked in with three Protectors. One word from me, and you'd be dead," he answers back. *Asshole.*

"Unlikely," Trex comments, and Seth narrows his eyes at him.

"This is why we don't treat demons fairly. They

can't be trusted to keep their word," Connor spits out.

"No, he is right. Bringing you here was a mistake, and in Seth's eyes, we are even," I say, frustrated.

"You came to Seth, and didn't even think to ask me? I'm offended, Vi," a familiar deep voice says before he steps out from the shadows in the corner of the room. Azi. My demon ex, and the very last person I want to see. I take a step back, narrowing my eyes on his red ones as he stops in the middle of the room. Azi hasn't changed a bit since I last saw him three years ago. Since he broke my heart, and I made sure he paid for it. His black hair is short, his pale skin still makes him look like a vampire or something, and his red eyes glow lightly. He has an expensive suit on, covering his muscular and impressive body that I used to love.

"What the fuck are you doing here?" I exclaim, my hand naturally going to my back where my dagger is.

"I heard you had some new, dangerous friends. I'm here to help with whatever trouble you have gotten yourself into," he says, grinning.

"Who is this?" Connor asks, placing his hand on

my arm to get my attention, and an audible growl comes from Azi.

"Just an ex, who I sent to Hell and hoped wouldn't return," I comment.

"Why did you send him to Hell?" Trex asks.

"We had a *mild* disagreement, and Evie took it too far," Azi drawls in an annoyed tone.

"Wait, let me get this straight. You sent your ex-boyfriend to Hell because you fell out with him?" Nix asks me, and I shrug.

"He shouldn't have been such an asshole," I reply, looking up see that very ex glaring at me from the other side of the room. I can't stop the smirk that appears on my lips. I'm damn proud of that day. Nix bursts into laughter, and when he stops, there is a tense silence to the room. Seth walks over to me, placing his hand on my shoulder.

"I cannot help you, but my brother can. Safe travels, Evie darling," he moves closer, whispering into my ear. "Change your mind about going to Hell, that is not where you should be. It's a death sentence for you." Seth pulls away and walks out of the room as I keep my eyes locked on Azi's.

"Why do you need to go to bottom layer of Hell?" Azi asks.

"None of your business," I state.

"It is if I'm taking you there," he replies.

"To rescue three very important people. Evie has made a deal, and the price—" I cut Connor off.

"-is Hali. They have Hali," I bite out, and Azi's eyes glow a brighter red. If veins start crawling down his face, I know he has lost control of his inner demon. I've only ever seen that happen once, and it was when he fell into Hell.

"Is she okay?" he asks, his hands in fists as he tries to calm down. I forget how much he cared for Hali. They were close before everything happened between us.

"The Protectors have promised her safety. I don't trust them, but we will have three hostages if they touch her," I point a thumb at the guys, who glare at me.

"Let me come with you, Vi. If not for you, then for Hali," he asks me. I stare at him for a second, before nodding my agreement.

"Fine," I say, knowing I'm going to regret this. "Meet us tomorrow morning at mine." Azi nods, before using one of his gifts to make flames smother him, and portal himself away.

"We should leave tonight," Trex demands as I turn and walk to the door.

"You are not dressed for Hell, for one, and two,

the top layer of Hell is the most dangerous at night," I say, and narrow my eyes at Trex.

"Why are you so desperate to go, more than Connor and your brother?" I ask.

"One of the princesses is his fiancé. Did they not tell you that?" Nix says, laughing low.

"Then we will get her back, but you have to do this *my* way," I say firmly. "And no more secrets. Hell is exactly that, hell. We have to have some trust between us all," I say and walk out of the room, swallowing the disappointment that the hot guy is engaged and off limits.

Chapter Twelve

EVIE

I PULL MY PLAIT UP INTO A BUN, WINDING IT AROUND and using hair slides to put it in place. I spent well over half an hour looking for the tiny little things. I always seem to lose when I need them. I pick the leather corset belt up off the bed, put it on, and tighten it up. I slide the five knives into their hidden compartments and make sure they are all secure before stepping away from the mirror. I glance at my bedroom; the clothes all over the floor, and the messy sheets from where I couldn't sleep last night. *How did everything change so quickly?* I fling the quiver full of arrows on my back, and my bag with food and water on the other side. I glance at myself in the mirror as I grab my bow and swallow the fear I have at going back to Hell. The last time was purely an accident, and I'll never forget it. The memory flashes in my mind without me even wanting to think about it.

I SCREAM AS I FALL INTO THE PORTAL AFTER THE Protector pushed me, and I keep falling as I open my eyes and spread my arms out to grab something. Snow and mountains are everywhere I look. The harsh snow slamming against my face as I fall makes me close my eyes again and hold my head to my chest. My body hits the snow-covered ground with a thud, sending pain shooting through what feels like every part of my body.

Where the hell am I? Antarctica? It certainly looks like it.

I stand up when I can, looking around at the empty area around me. There is nothing but snow, and well, more snow. I look up at the sky, pausing when I can't see the sun, or the moon. There are no stars, just blackness with a blue smoky haze that gives off light. Right, time to leave. I pull my sleeve up, pressing my finger to my red rune and try to call a portal.

Nothing happens.

That's impossible.

The rune doesn't even glow red. I move to my other arm, pulling the sleeve up in a panic and pressing my finger against the blue rune. My hand instantly burns with holy blue fire. So that rune works here. I close my hand, putting out the fire and looking around again. I spot a fire in the distance to my right, and I start walking towards it, crawling to get over the hill. When I get to the top, I freeze at the horror in front of me. There are hundreds, maybe even thousands, of demons walking in a line, with transparent-looking people in the middle of them. The people look human, but it's hard to tell from where I am. They are see-through, though, and that's not normal.

"What do we have here?" I hear a sickening sounding voice say from behind me, and I turn, seeing a demon that looks half snake and half human in front of me. I step back, missing my step, and I go tumbling down the hill.

The next three days the demons keep me, feeding off my blood and beating me senseless. It's all a blur, but I have never been as powerless as I am now. The next real thing I am aware of is a red, a bright light...When I open my eyes, a red-eyed demon with black hair and a handsome face is holding me in his hands.

"You're safe now."

I SNAP OUT OF THE THE MEMORY OF THE fIRST TIME I met Azi, and the only time I've ever been to Hell. I saw a lot of it as the demons dragged me around as their slave. They claimed my blood was worth more than any they had ever seen, and that it was the only reason they didn't kill me. I walk out of my bedroom, closing the door behind me. Azi may have saved me, but he broke me far worse than any demon did in Hell. *He should have left me there.* I stare around at the empty apartment; the stillness of it, and I hate it. I hate being in my home without Hali. It's too quiet, and it's too messy. Hali was the neat freak, and I tend to forget to pick my stuff up. I used to get annoyed when she moved stuff to clean, and I couldn't find it, but now I miss having her around to do that. *It's only been two days, and I will get her back.* I have to keep telling myself that, or I might lose the plot and try to rescue her instead of moving forward with this plan. I go to the kitchen, reaching into the fridge, and getting out my five packets of bacon when I smell a familiar smoky scent, and then I sense him. I turn around to see Azi standing in my living room, with only the faint trails of smoke still surrounding him to tell me he used a portal to get in here. He is dressed for Hell this time, no more suits like he usually wears. This time he has a North Face jacket on, similar to mine, but his is blue. He has a bag on his back, two swords, and I'm sure plenty of other weapons hidden underneath. I hate the first moment I see him, my body instantly warms, remembering every moment we spent together like it was yesterday. He was my first everything, and being with him was the first time I felt safe. *But he ruined it, and I have to remember that.*

"Have you heard of knocking?" I frown at him, pulling my bag off my back, and shoving my bacon in the container inside. It won't last more than a couple days, but the freezing landscape should help keep the bacon fresh.

"Bacon? I see you haven't changed much in all these years," he chuckles as I close my bag and chuck it on my shoulder. I ignore him, starting to walk to the door, but he steps in my way, making me arch my neck to look up at him.

"Get out of the way," I snap, and he continues to move closer, until he's close enough that I can smell his peppermint scent. I never knew if it was a cologne, or something he put on that made him smell that way, but I always loved how he smelt.

"We need to talk, what happened–"

"I don't want to talk about it. You fucked me over, just like everyone said you would. Demons like you can't be trusted, and they certainly can't love anyone but themselves. So, get the fuck out of my way before I do something that *you* will regret," I threaten him as his eyes burn with anger, and he goes to reply when there is a knock at the door.

"Come in," I say, stepping back, and Azi steps aside.

"This isn't over, and if I have to tie you down to make you talk to me, I will," he states firmly, crossing his arms with a determined expression. I hate that he knows I like being tied up. Can't believe the bastard actually just used that against me.

"You can try," I harshly whisper just as the door opens and the Protectors walk in. They have cloaks on again, this time with rucksacks on their backs, and weapons everywhere to be seen. I notice straight away the two axes on Trex's back. The shiny black metal looks awesome. Connor has swords, and when he walks over, I spot the dozens of daggers and two guns on his belt. Nix is the last one through the door, and he doesn't look impressed, but he does look hot. He has a bow, similar to mine, attached to his back along with arrows.

"Here, these are for you and Azi. They have advanced Protector's technology in them, making them stay as warm as you need them," Connor offers me the folded-up cloaks. I nod, accepting them and chucking one at Azi, who catches it.

"Where is it safe to make a portal around here?" Trex asks as I take my supplies and clip the cloak on. I put everything back on and pick up my bow.

"There is a basement under the building. It's big enough, and no one goes in it," I reply, pushing past them all and towards the door. They follow me down the steps, and I wait for them to leave the house before locking the door. I walk around the building to the alleyway, unlocking the basement door with my key and walking down the steps. I wait until we are all in the middle of the dark basement, with Connor using the flashlight on his phone to see. The others don't care, and Azi can see in the dark, anyway.

"Are you ready for this?" I ask, pulling an arrow out my quiver and holding it at my side. They all nod, pulling their weapons out. Azi doesn't, he just stands still.

"Are you opening the portal, or me?" Azi asks.

"Me. Just keep an eye out, we can't have any souls escaping. You know how much trouble souls can cause humans. People don't like ghosts, and we haven't got time to call a reaper," I comment, and pull my sleeve up, pressing my finger to my red rune and thinking of Hell. I open my eyes as my rune glows bright, blasting red light into the room. A second later, a red portal burns into existence, getting bigger and bigger until it's about the size of a door. A soul rushes out almost instantly, and I load my bow, shooting it in the chest, and sending it back through the door.

"After you," I say, waving my hand at the door. Connor runs into it first, followed by Nix and Trex.

"I'm going last," Azi tells me, and I don't bother arguing with him, running towards the portal and jumping in, feeling the fire burn all over me, and then I'm just falling.

Chapter Thirteen

EVIE

I LAND WITH A ROLL WHEN I FALL OUT OF THE portal, and bump into someone, knocking myself onto my side. I sit up, seeing Connor on the floor, shaking his head as he gets up. Nix and Trex are slowly standing up, looking a bit dazed, but at least they didn't break anything on the floor. I stand up quickly, loading my arrow into my bow and looking around while they aren't focused. Travelling great distances in portals can make you feel a little drunk sometimes, and I've travelled through so many it doesn't bother me anymore. I doubt it will bother Azi, either, when he finally manages to get his ass down here. I look around, not seeing anyone or anything near us. It's just snow, and the mountains behind us. At the sound of a loud bang, I turn around to see Azi land in a crouch, and he grins at me before rising to stand.

"Where to next?" Connor asks, walking over to me. He brushes snow out of his hair as the others come over.

"See the mountains there," I point to them as I speak. "They hold the entrance to the next layer. It's not going to be easy to get to them, but once we are inside it's only demons we have to deal with," I tell them, and they give me a confused look.

"The souls here are the worst of any souls. They are stuck here for their actions in their lives, and the demons usually feed off them until they fade away. They aren't like souls on Earth, who have to put a lot of energy into just moving a flower pot or something," I explain.

"And the good souls? What happens to them? Are they here?" Nix asks.

"Truly good souls never come to Hell. Souls that are neutral are taken to the second layer, and reborn," Azi explains for me, and Nix nods, looking away sharply. *What was that about?*

"Let's go, it's going to take us at least seven hours on foot to reach the mountains. And that's only if we don't run into trouble along the way," I say, putting my bow back on my back and walking ahead. We walk in silence for about an hour, and I'm impressed with how well the Protectors are able to keep up with me. They don't complain about the climbing in the snow, or the fact the temperature is dropping every hour. The snow is beginning to freeze over and become hard to walk on. Nix catches up to me, while the others are closer together just behind us.

"Can I ask you something, love?" Nix asks, grabbing my arm when I nearly slip on some ice. I pull my arm away, meeting his light-green eyes that don't seem to have a motive.

"I might answer, so you might as well ask," I reply eventually.

"How old were you when you killed someone for the first time?" he asks.

"Why? Do you want to know how long I've been a monster?" I snap out in reply, and he shakes his head, his black hair moving with him and getting some of the snow out of it.

"If killing as a child, when you had no choice, makes you a monster . . . well, that makes me one, too," he admits, making me pause for second, and look at him.

"How old were you?" I ask.

"Five. I killed my father," he responds in a cold

tone. I *knew* there was something dark about him. This kind of explains some things.

"Why?" I reply.

"For beating up and killing my mother. He was about to kill Trex, holding a dagger dripping with my mother's blood to his throat. I picked up one of his daggers off the floor, where he had dropped it, and slammed it into his cold, dead heart," he tells me the story like it isn't something that happened to him. There is no real emotion in his retelling of the story. That must be his way of coping, pretending that his past happened to someone else. *I don't blame him.*

"You don't seem to regret it," I reply.

"I don't," he says firmly.

"You shouldn't, and I am sorry," I tell him honestly.

"I told you. Now, shouldn't you tell me your story in return, love?" he asks. I want to ignore him, but something makes me speak instead.

"I was eight, older than you," I start off.

"Who was it?" he asks.

"A Protector. I had left the demon compound, ignoring my friend's advice, and thinking I knew better. Thinking I was safe . . . but I wasn't. He was waiting for me," I say, trying to forget the fear I felt when the Protector caught me, and slammed me onto the ground, holding a dagger to my neck. I wasn't a fighter back then, just a scared child.

"How did an eight-year-old beat an adult Protector?" he enquires.

"My friend was a witch, and a smart one. She was older than me, eighteen at the time I was attacked. She had just gotten her power and followed me to make sure I was safe for the night. She used her gifts to hold the Protector down, and I killed him with the dagger he tried to kill me with," I tell him, trying to keep any emotion out of my voice. She also suggested leaving my rune name on him as a way of scaring the other Protectors away. It became a thing I just did after a while.

"Where is your friend now?" Nix asks.

"She died," I reply simply, still missing her with every single part of me, and I can't even say her name now. It hurts too much. I stop dead in my tracks, hearing a slight sound, seconds before over twenty souls rush at us from all directions. We walked straight into a soul trap. The souls appear almost see through, but any weapon with silver on it will kill them. Luckily all my weapons have silver, but there are a lot of them, and not enough of us.

"Weapons, now!" I shout, pulling my bow off

and grabbing an arrow. Nix does the same, and we start firing instantly. I hit three souls before they get too close and whack the nearest one with the end of my bow when it heads towards me. I grab a dagger out of my belt, slamming it into the soul of what looks like a burnt body as it runs at me. I turn around, just in time to see Trex slam his axe over the head of a soul.

"Shit, there are too many. It's like they have gathered together to find us and trap us," I mutter, grabbing the hand of the soul that reaches for me, and flipping it over my shoulder, slamming my dagger into it as it lands. I jump up, looking around, and seeing nothing but souls. More and more are running towards us, far more than the twenty we started with. Crap a doodle.

"Azi!" I shout at him, seeing him holding two souls in his hands, and he is burning them. He quickly kills them, looking over at me, and then to the army surrounding us.

"Alright," he shouts. "Cover me!"

"Everyone cover Azi, and jump into the flame portal he makes!" I tell them, neglecting to mention that it hurts like hell to go through a demon portal. It will likely knock us all out, including Azi for holding it open so long. The guys do as I ask, and I pull another arrow out, shooting soul after soul as I back up. I get to Azi's side just as he opens the fire portal, which looks just like a wall of flames. Connor gives me a wide-eyed look, but I don't have time to look at the others as a soul runs at Nix, catching him off guard, and biting his arm. He swears, pulling the soul off of him, and I shoot the soul with an arrow. He holds his arm as he backs towards the portal and jumps in with a nod at me.

"Jump in Connor, Trex! Azi can't hold it for long!" I say, knowing I'm close to leaving their asses here. Connor jumps in, and Trex kills two more souls with his axe before jumping.

"*Now*, Vi!" Azi says, sweat pouring down his forehead, and his red eyes blazing. I put my finger to my blue rune, calling my holy fire and make a wall of it in front of us, seeing the souls run towards the holy fire, and burning themselves. I turn around, and run into the portal, feeling like every part of me is burning before I land somewhere cold, then black out.

Chapter Fourteen

EVIE

"*Evie . . .*" I hear my friend speak, her words filled with shock as I pull the dagger out of the chest of the Protector on the floor.

"*He was waiting for me in here. He knew I would come to see you today and get food,*" I say with a shaky voice, my hand dropping the dagger onto the ground as I realise what I've done. I've killed him.

"*Don't you dare feel guilty, not for this. I'm sorry I wasn't here to protect you until the end,*" she says, coming over to me.

"*Why do they keep coming for me? Why am I not safe anywhere? I thought this place was safe?*" I ask. I was lucky to kill this one, and if I hadn't been training with the old demon I found to help me, I wouldn't have survived. And if she hadn't come home, and stopped him with her magic...

"I thought the same, but evidently, it's not. We will move to another place," she states, holding her hands on her hips and staring at the dead Protector.

"I can just leave by myself. You don't have to move because of me. If I'm not here, they won't come after you," I say, trying not to look as upset as I feel.

"I'm not leaving an eight-year-old on the streets while she is hunted by monsters. Even a smart eight-year-old like you," she says, tutting like she does when she isn't happy.

"But you're a witch; you can't leave your people," I protest. All the witches live in this demon underground. They own the section my friend lives in.

"I have no living family, and I'm a teacher, so I can get a job anywhere," she reminds me, and I nod, biting my lip. "The witches won't miss me, don't worry."

"What should we do with him?" I ask, knowing we can't just leave him here. My friend picks a picture up off the side, the drawing of my rune name I drew earlier today when I was bored.

"We leave this, as a warning for whoever is after you," she says, leaning down and placing the drawing on his chest. "Now help me pack our stuff, and no more living on the streets for you. You can hide with me, and we will figure something out. I'm tired of letting you walk out that door for nights on end and worrying as I wait for you to come back, Evie."

"You're like the only real family I've ever had," I say
quietly.

"Not 'like', we are family," she says, pulling me into her
arms and kissing my forehead. "You won't be alone ever
again, Evie."

"VI, WAKE UP," AZI'S VOICE PENETRATES THROUGH
the darkness, and I blink my eyes open. As everything comes into focus, I notice my head is in his
lap, and his hand is gently stroking my cheek. For a
second, I forget what happened in the past, only
seeing his handsome features and the red eyes that
would scare most, but not me. They've never scared
me. I have always liked the darkness. The emotion I
can see in his eyes now calls to me. I'm not sure if
it's real, but I don't know if I can look away. "Vi, I
never meant to hurt you. It was always you for me,
from the moment I met you here. Let me explain
what happened that night."

"Azi," I whisper softly, and the sound of a male
groan snaps me out of whatever moment we were
having. I jump off his lap, ignoring his annoyed
glare. I can't risk letting him close like that again.
This is a job, that's all. *That was stupid, Evie.* I pull
myself to my feet, looking around at the small cave

we are in and the snow just outside the entrance. By the looks of the trail of snow, Azi dragged us in here from outside. I look over to see Trex waking up, shaking his head and looking dazed. *Where the hell are we?*

"I'm going to get some wood, or anything we can use. I checked the cave while I waited for you to wake up, and it is safe. It's night, and we aren't going anywhere until morning," he pauses. "We are at the bottom of the mountain to answer your unasked question," Azi says, pulling his cloak around him, and walking out of the cave without another word.

"What happened?" Connor mumbles, sitting up–his gold hair sticking up all over the place, and he has mud all over his cheek. He rubs his face, glancing at his friends and pulling his bag off his back, getting out a drink. Trex is still struggling to come around, running his hands over his face. I try to hide my smile when he looks my way, but he sees it anyway. I chuckle and look back at Connor.

"Demon portals aren't made for anything other than demons. When our kind travels through, it knocks us out. It can kill humans if they travel too far in them," I tell him as he drinks some water and shakes his head at me.

"You could have mentioned that *before* we went through the portal!" Trex snaps, going over to his brother, and shaking his shoulder. Nix groggily slaps Trex's hand away as he wakes up, looking around the room and falling back with a dramatic groan.

"Oh, I'm sorry. Next time, I will leave you with the souls and let them eat you, you ungrateful asshole!" I snap right back at Trex, and his eyes burn with hate and anger as he stands up to walk over, but Connor steps in front of him.

"She is right. We didn't have a choice and would be dead if Azi hadn't opened the portal. Let's make camp, rather than try to kill each other. We have enough dangerous obstacles ahead that will attempt to maim and murder us. Remember why we are here, Trex," Connor suggests, but Trex doesn't take his furious eyes off me.

"Fine," he finally spits out, turning around, and going over to his brother. *At least the asshole listens to someone.* I take my bag off, pulling out my blanket first and putting it on the ground. I lay my weapons next to it, keeping my daggers on my thighs just in case.

"He isn't waking up," I hear Trex say, and I look over to see him shaking Nix's shoulder, and Connor kneeling down next to them. *Shit, he got bit.*

"He was bit by a soul on his arm," I say, standing up, "Nix needs the poison sucked out and the wound disinfected," I tell them, and they both dart their eyes to me.

"Sucked out?" Trex asks with a disgusted frown.

"Boys," I roll my eyes at them and walk over, nudging Connor out of the way. I begin to lift Nix's arm, but Trex grabs my wrist, stopping me. I look up, meeting his dark-green eyes. "Why can't you use your white rune to heal him?"

"Runes don't work on the dead, or anything they infect. I know this, I've seen people try. Nix *will* die if we don't get the poison out," I tell him firmly. I've seen it happen so many times in the demon underground. People who ventured into hell for whatever reason and escaped with bites, thinking they were free. This is the only way to save people, the only way I've seen work. I was lucky demons found me when I fell into the Hell, and the souls didn't get near me. Not that what the demons did was any better. I remember praying for death at times, and the souls could have given me that.

"I can help, I want to help him . . . so let me?" I ask him, as gently as I can make myself speak. He watches me for a second, before letting go.

"If my brother dies, I will hold you responsible," he growls.

"I get it. I'm pretty sure this is the second time you have threatened to kill me, and yet, here I am. If I was going to betray you, I would have done it by now," I tell him, looking down at Nix's arm, and pulling the sleeve up. The bite itself isn't too bad, but the poison from the dead soul is crawling through his veins near the bite. I can see it spreading underneath the tattoos that cover his arm, right up to his wrist. The bite is in-between the blue and black runes on his arm. I turn it over and see his rune name written down the side of his arm, hidden in all the other tattoos.

"He wouldn't want you to know his name," Trex tells me.

"I can't read runes, so I won't know it," I tell him, and he gives me a questioning look. I'm sure he has a million questions to ask, but he doesn't voice any of them. The room is deadly silent as I kneel down, getting ready.

"Can you do this? He is my brother; I can do this if you can't," Trex tells me firmly.

"I've done worse to save someone I like . . . plus, I've seen this done a few times. I know when to stop, and when to wash the poison out of my mouth when it starts burning," I tell him, he doesn't reply, but he seems to get the idea that I am trying to help his brother.

"Connor, go in my bag, and get the bottle of vodka out. We will need it," I tell him, and he nods sharply, running over to my bag.

"If he wakes up and tries to fight me off, you need to stop him. Understood?" I ask Trex, who nods, leaning closer and getting ready. "This will hurt." I say to the unconscious Nix before covering my mouth over the bite and beginning to suckthe poison out. I alternate sucking and spitting out the poison, and keep an eye on his arm, watching the veins turning back to normal slowly. It takes about twenty minutes of this before Nix wakes up with a start. His natural reaction is as I predicted it would be, and he immediately tries to push me away. Trex holds him down, but he seems to struggle a bit as his brother goes mad.

"Evie is helping you, relax," Trex soothes him in a firm tone. Nix calms down a little before looking up at me with a grin.

"Sucking me already? We haven't even gone on a date yet, love," he flirts even when he must be in a lot of pain. I pull my mouth away, spitting out the last of the poison.

"You'll have to return the favour sometime," I say, smirking as I wink at him. Connor quickly hands me the bottle of vodka, and I drink some, washing my mouth out and spitting out the last of the poison. I quickly pour some on the cut, making Nix hiss, but he doesn't stop me.

"Consider it a promise," Nix replies, his voice tired. Connor hands me a bandage, and I quickly wrap Nix's arm, pushing him down when he tries to sit up.

"Rest, we have about six hours until the morning, and we can't leave at night," I explain to them, grabbing the bottle of vodka off the floor. Nix holds his good arm out for the bottle, and I hand it to him, watching him guzzle some before he hands it back to me. I drink some more before putting the lid back on.

"Azi is getting wood for a fire, and we will have to take turns on watch. That army of souls was not normal; they don't travel together like that. I have a feeling whoever took your princesses has told the souls to kill us and offered them something," I state, and none of them say anything, but the way they exchange quick glances lets me know they are thinking the same thing. "Let's hope it's only souls they have after us. There are much worse things in

Hell to send to kill someone." I walk to edge of the cave before they can reply to me. Slipping a dagger from its sheath, I sit and watch for Azi to come back, or for anything dangerous lurking in the snow. *Whoever has the princesses does not want them found.*

Chapter Fifteen

NIX

"HEY," I SAY, HANDING EVIE A PROTEIN BAR AND sitting down next to her. She looks at the bar in her hand, before she shrugs and opens it up.

"You should be resting," she says, not looking at me but still keeping an eye out. Azi came back an hour ago and set the fire up with our help. We have three tents set up in the cave around the fire. Azi offered to swap with Evie, but she didn't want to and told him to sleep in case we need another portal. It's clear something bad happened between them, though they clearly still have feelings for each other. Or, at least, Azi does. I'm not sure about Evie. She turns to look at me, her bright-blue eyes reflecting the light from the fire in the cave, and it makes her look so very innocent and stunning. She may be stunning, but we all know innocent isn't a word that can be used to describe her. She has let her hair down, and it frames her face. The dark blue is stunning, so natural and like it was always meant to be that colour.

"I needed some fresh air," I tell her, pulling out my own protein bar from my coat and opening it. I bite down on the chewy crap, hating the fake plastic taste.

"These are crap," Evie voices my thoughts on the bar, scrunching her face up and putting the bar down after she chews a bit.

"Crap is a nice word for it," I say.

"How does your arm feel?" she asks, not exactly concerned, but more curious.

"Better. I'm alive, and I owe you for it," I respond, keeping my eyes locked on hers. I will pay her back for the debt one day. I will never forget what she did for me.

"Can I sit?" Connor asks from behind me. His question is clearly for Evie more than it was for me, judging from the way he stares at her.

"I don't own Hll, you can sit wherever you like, Connor," she replies, and he chuckles, going to her other side and sitting down.

"You both should be sleeping," she comments.

"If you keep telling me to go to bed, love, I might start getting excited that you're going to join me," I tease her, watching how she turns to look at me with a small grin.

"You're such a flirt, Nix," she says with a low chuckle, and looks back into the cave.

"Is Azi really your ex?" Connor blurts out, his gaze following to where she is looking. Her whole face tightens with her fists as she looks back at the entrance.

"Yes," she replies dryly.

"You really dated a demon? A demon *overlord?*" Connor asks in shock. Evie laughs, shaking her head.

"Demons aren't all that different from humans and Protectors," she tells us. I've lost count of how many demons I have killed, how many I've sent back to Hell on missions. Demons aren't all roses and sunshine, that's for sure. I'm certain Azi has done his fair share of evil things.

"You know he is an overlord? Do Protectors even know much about overlords?" she asks us.

"We know there are ten overlords, all brothers. All very powerful, and that our old king killed one over three hundred years ago," I tell her, and she nods her head.

"Azi said his brother deserved to die, that his sin was controlling him and making him evil. Though, I still wouldn't bring up his brother again," she suggests.

"Sin?" I ask.

"Each brother has a sin that makes them an overlord. Think of the seven deadly sins, and you get a rough idea," she shrugs.

"What is Azi's?" I ask.

"Not my secret to tell," she replies quickly, with a little smirk on her soft, pretty, heart-shaped lips.

"You protect him, even though he clearly hurt you. What happened?" I ask.

"Why should I tell you?" she sharply questions in return.

"We are likely to die down here, so anything you tell us will be kept secret," Connor says, making her laugh.

"I've seen you all fight, you might not die down here," she says. *That was almost a compliment.* She might be starting to like us, after all.

"Then we will keep our mouths shut, so the big, bad, deadly assassin doesn't come after us," I tease her, and she laughs, but it dies off. We are silent for a while before she starts speaking.

"Azi saved me from Hell when I was eighteen. I

fell in here by accident when I was fighting a Protector. I think he was trying to send me here, anyway," she says, clearing her throat as my fists tighten in anger for her. *A Protector came after a child? Why the hell would they do that?* "Azi and I hit it off instantly, and I fell for him. I was young and stupid, and he was hot, knowledgeable, and well, off-limits being a demon overlord and all. I have always liked the dangerous shit in life. He was just different from anyone I had met. I trusted him," she stops, anger burning over her eyes.

"So, what happened to make you hate him like you do now?" Connor asks gently.

"I walked into our apartment, seeing him with a half-naked demon girl standing between his legs as he sat on a chair. I opened a portal to hell and made sure they both went into it. I haven't talked to him until the club the other day," she tells us.

"Then, he is a fucking idiot, Blue. If he had you, he had something he never should have thrown away," Connor tells her, and she laughs.

"I know, and he knows that now. I'm sure when he came back to his apartment to see all his designer clothes cut up, and all his expensive shit destroyed, he realised his mistake," she says, and I laugh.

"I bet that annoyed him," Connor laughs.

"It did, but I was more bothered about other things at the time. Vi also stole my lucky cat statue, which I want back, by the way. Can we talk, Vi?" Azi asks from behind us, and Evie stands up.

"Stop calling me Vi, and you're *never* getting your cat statue back," she snaps and walks around him as his glowing red eyes fill the cave with light. "I'm going to nap." We all watch her walk away until she disappears into the cave.

"Don't even think about touching her. She is mine," Azi states, placing his hands on his hips. I laugh as I stand up, walking over, so we are eye to eye.

"She sent you to Hell, which you deserved. You don't stand a chance, and she fucking isn't yours. She is a Protector," I tell him, watching him slowly begin to lose his temper. Connor places his hand on my shoulder, pulling me away.

"Evie doesn't belong to anyone, not the Protectors and not the demons. I can tell that from just knowing her a few days," Connor tells us both. "This alpha macho shit won't get you back in her good graces, Azi," he tells Azi, and then walks away from us both to the cave entrance.

"I'm watching, go and sleep," Connor tells me. I

pull my eyes away from Azi's, walking around him. I'm surprised when he doesn't say a word to me, but maybe he can't because he knows Connor's right. Evie isn't anyone's. But I like her, and I'm damn well going to try to make her notice me. *Evie is worth pissing off a demon for.*

Chapter Sixteen

EVIE

"IS THAT BACON?" CONNOR ASKS, GROGGILY waking up from his nap, and his tired eyes meet mine. He looks like a cute lion teddy in the morning, with his messy gold hair, and his gold eyes look brighter somehow. I clear my throat, looking back at my pan as I cook the bacon.

"Yes, *my* bacon," I explain to him tartly. I look around at Azi and Nix talking by the door and to Trex who is resting his back against a wall, watching me like a hawk. He acts like I'm about to try and stab him or something. I mean it's not a move far from my mind, because he *is* an ass, but I care more about my bacon at the moment.

"She doesn't share bacon, man. She would most

likely stab you for even attempting to touch it," Azi warns Connor, who chuckles.

"I hate to admit it, but he is right. I don't share bacon, not with *anyone*," I say seriously and Connor grins, standing up. I watch as he stretches, his arms lifting above his head and raising his shirt to show off his flat, toned stomach. My eyes can't help but follow the trail of golden hair that leads from his stomach and into his trousers. *I wonder if the carpet matches the drapes?* I pull my eyes away from Connor to see Azi glaring at me, his eyes drifting between me and Connor.

"Connor, we need to have a look around, see if we can spot an entrance to the mountains. Come with Nix and me. Evie and Trex can stay here and keep watch," Azi demands, picking up his sword and walking out of the cave. Connor laughs, clearly picking up on Azi's jealousy as he leans closer to me.

"See you in a bit, Blue," he twirls a bit of my blue hair around his finger, making me wonder if he is an idiot or perhaps he's just a brave idiot. Connor then grabs his sword and coat, shooting me a smirk and wink, before walking out. There's an awkward silence as I finish cooking my bacon. I savor it, eating the bacon slowly, before I clean my pot and put it back in my bag.

"Why do I have the feeling you are going to try and attack me, Trexy?" I ask him, knowing he is thinking about it. The way he has been watching me, and the dagger hidden in his right hand, tells me all I need to know.

"What the fuck did you just call me?" he growls.

"Trexy . . . it suits you, I think," I chuckle, standing up as he does. We walk in sync with each other in circles. At least he isn't pretending he doesn't want to kill me.

"Trying to kill me now is your best option. The others will be back soon, and they won't let you attempt it," I say, wanting to get this over with. He does exactly what I thought he would, and runs straight at me. I dive under his dagger-holding arm, grabbing his wrist and twisting. He drops the dagger and I grab it quickly, kicking his back to make him stumble. He turns around, glaring at me.

"Is that what they teach you at Protector school? If so, no wonder you guys are so easy to kill," I say honestly, and he runs at me again. I chuckle, running as well and diving onto the floor, skidding across and grabbing his leg, bringing him to the floor. He grabs me, trying to pull me to him, and I let him for second, before kicking his face with my boot and jumping on him, pressing the dagger to his throat. He watches me carefully with his dirt-smothered face, and his green eyes that are far prettier up close. He is more gorgeous than I thought now that I'm closer to him. *Shame about the whole hating me and being engaged thing.*

"Why the fuck do you hate me so much, Trex?" I ask him, honestly wanting to know why.

"You killed my uncle. I was eleven when they dragged his body to our home. He was my uncle, and you murdered him," he growls.

"I was and still am hunted. I've never had another option; it's kill or be killed. Think about it. We aren't all that different in age, I was obviously only a child myself when your uncle tried to kill me. *You know what's worse?* I don't even remember him, just another Protector that came after me. I don't like to kill but I had, and still have, no choice," I tell him.

"You do like to kill, it's who you are. I can see it your cold eyes," he chuckles darkly.

"You don't know a thing, Trexy," I bite back, holding the dagger closer, trying to resist the urge to kill the bastard and prove him right.

"Go on, do it. Be the assassin, the killer we all

know you are," Trex taunts me. I move my legs closer around his waist and lean down, pressing my lips close to his, but not quite close enough to touch. His whole body goes tense as his eyes burn with anger.

"That's the funny thing, though . . . you don't know a thing about me," I reply sweetly.

"I know you kill anyone that gets in your way, and I know your name is whispered in fear by every Protector," he spits out, and I lean back with a dramatic sigh.

"Then you don't know me at all. I never kill anyone that hasn't tried to kill me first. Maybe you should get your facts straight before trying to attack me again, Trex," I say with a smirk as his eyes widen in disbelief. Of course, he would never believe that his precious, stuck-up race would send their soldiers to kill me. I chuckle, moving my knife away and climbing off of him as I hear footsteps. Connor walks in, covered in black slime and stops in his tracks as he stares at us. Even covered in disgusting-smelling crap, he looks hotter than he should.

"We have a big fucking problem, so stop flirting, and get the hell outside to help," he shouts and then walks straight back out. I run and grab my weapons and my bow before running out of the cave. The sight that greets me stops me in my tracks. Azi, Connor, and Nix fighting with massive, green, disgusting-looking creatures. They are dripping with green slime looking stuff. The only part of them describable is their black eyes and long mouths full of spikes instead of teeth.

"What the hell are those?" Trex asks in shock.

"Get back!" I shout at the guys as I pull my sleeve up and call my blue rune. Once Connor, Azi, and Nix are at my side, I make a wall of holy fire, which burns out when the creatures run at it.

"Azi, have you ever seen anything like that?" I ask him in shock, and he shakes his head, running his hands through his hair.

"No, but I don't want to stick around to make more explode. They stink," Azi says, and I just now notice that all of them are covered in the green slime. *And they stink.*

"I found a trail, this way," Nix points to our right to a small path through the caves that leads up the mountains by the looks of it.

"Brilliant, let's go," I say, looking back at the creatures once more before walking up the path after getting our bags.

Chapter Seventeen

EVIE

"WE ARE GETTING CLOSE TO THE GATE FOR THE next level," Azi tells us as we continue to climb. I stop, needing a break like everyone else seems to as I look back at them. We have been climbing straight uphill for over five hours, with the freezing cold wind and harsh snow. Every part of me is freezing, and thank god for the thermal gloves I am wearing, or I'm sure I would have lost my fingers already.

"Time for a drink," I say, holding my hand up so they all stop. I lean against a slab of rock, pulling my drink bottle out of my bag, only to see that's it's frozen solid.

"Fuck," I mutter, struggling to even get the bottle's lid off. Two hands cover mine on the bottle, gently warming up slowly. Azi doesn't say a word as he defrosts the bottle and steps away.

"Thanks," I nod at him and he smiles in response, almost sadly.

"Dude, I could use some help with that trick," Connor says, and Azi just scowls at him, walking away a little. "Asshole."

I drink half my water with a smile and then walk over to Connor, handing him my bottle.

"That's yours," he insists, and I push it at him.

"I don't need anymore," I say, and walk back to my spot, leaning against the slab of rock. I quickly scarf down a breakfast bar out of my bag and wait for the others before we start walking again. The end of the path finally comes into view, and the massive cavern.

"The gate," Azi shouts, but his voice is lost in the wind. I pause when a burning scent hits me, and I hold my hand up to make the others stop as I slide a dagger out of my belt.

"What?" Connor asks, and I look back at them for a second, placing my finger on my lips. I've only smelt that kind of burning once, and if one of those demons are around, we are in *deep* shit. I keep my footsteps as silent and light as I can as I run to the edge of the path, hiding behind the rocks. The others do the same, staying close to the rocks as I edge my head around. Peering around the rock, I see the very type of demon I never wanted to see again, along with two of its friends, standing at the cave entrance. *Gragnog demons.* Gragnog demons have bodies similar to ours, but they are constantly on fire, and their hands are two long, sharp bones instead of hands. They have one eye on their head, and a mouth full of sharp teeth, but their appearance isn't the worst thing about them. They feed on burning–burning humans mainly. One touch of their fire against your skin makes you feel like you're dying, and it makes them feel like they've had an energy drink.

"Shit," I whisper as I lean back and look at the others.

"What?" Azi demands.

"Gragnog demons. One adult and two teen ones by the looks of them. They are waiting, most likely for us," I snap out, glaring at the Protectors because this is clearly all their fault.

"We will have to go around," Nix states.

"We don't have time for that. We need to get to the next layer, not travel around the fucking mountain. It's three against five, we can do this," Trex says, and steps out before I can grab him.

"You are a complete fucking idiot," I hiss, as the demons turn to us.

"Maybe," he grins. "Let's see how deadly the legendary assassin is, huh?"

I don't have time to reply to the idiot as the demons run at us, and I throw my dagger straight at the biggest one. He has his eyes locked on me as the dagger hits his chest, and it doesn't even seem to faze him. One of the younger ones goes for Connor and Trex, and Nix is left with the other. I go to fight the big demon when Azi jumps in front of me.

"New plan, get in the cave and dive into the water!" Azi shouts, grabbing one of the demons, and holding him in the air. Azi somehow manages to keep control of the older one by holding the demon's sharp hands behind his back. I run to the younger demon fighting Nix, burning his chest as he pushes him against a rock with one of his dagger arms. I lean around the demon, grabbing Nix's fallen sword from the ground. I grab the demon's shoulder, ignoring the heat burning my gloves. I hastily swing the sword hard across his neck, cutting off its head, and it falls to the ground with a bounce. *Gross.*

"Nihil!" the demon Azi is holding screams as his

friend dies. I lock eyes with Azi while the demon continues its struggle to get free.

"Run, I will portal to find you!" Azi demands, and I turn around, grabbing Nix's arm and pulling him towards the cave entrance. I see Connor and Trex finish off their demon, before running after us. The cave entrance is tiny, with a ledge that over-looks a very fast-paced, and deep-looking river. The river has a waterfall at the other end; it appears to be a large one, by the looks of it.

"Fuck it," I grumble, running to the ledge and jumping off the cliff into the freezing-cold water.

Chapter Eighteen

EVIE

I GASP FOR AIR AS MY HEAD BURSTS OUT OF THE water, and into the cold air that feels like it burns my lungs. The river pulls me too fast down it, way too fast for me to be able to swim or control where I'm going. The current pushes me around as I try to look for anything to grab onto. My head goes under again with the strength of the current, and I try to move my arms to get my head above the water again when my arm hits something, cutting me, and I feel pain reel through my arm as I feel a snap. I struggle in the river, more water filling my lungs as I try to swim up. An arm hooks around my waist suddenly, pulling me up, and I gasp again, finally able to suck in air.

"Hold on to me, love. I got you," Nix's voice

says next to my ear, his warm breath relaxing me. I turn in his arms, seeing a yellow vest jacket that is full of air on his chest, holding him above the water. I wrap my legs around his chest, and use my hands to grip on his bag straps on his shoulders as the river rushes us towards the waterfall. My arm stings with the pain from the movement, but I don't have time to think about it as I stare at him. There isn't anything to grab hold of, or anyone around us either. *Where are Trex and Connor?*

"Thanks," I mumble to him, and he rests his forehead against mine. I give him a confused look, which he only grins at as water splashes against us.

"We are about to fall off a waterfall and likely die. I want to hold the hottest girl in the world before that happens. It will give me a good memory to die with," he explains with a cheeky grin.

"Charmer," I mutter with a laugh, and then I lean forward, pressing my lips to his cold ones. He groans, kissing me back fervently. The kiss seems like a goodbye, a sweet seductive one, and he moves away only seconds before we fall off the edge of the waterfall. I have to let go, only seeing his green eyes blaze as he reaches for me, but the water takes me instead.

***

Coughing as I come to, I slowly blink my eyes open and try to get my bearings. I can see nothing but the top of a cave, which has gaps that light the interior, and only hear rushing water in the distance. I can feel I'm lying on little wet rocks, the gravel sticks to my fingers as I sit up. I cry out when I put weight on my left arm to push myself up, and remember hurting it in the river. I look around, seeing the waterfall and nothing other than the beach I am on. *Where are the Protectors?*

"Are you hurt?" Trex's gruff voice comes from behind me, and I turn around to see him picking himself up off the ground. I spot Connor on the ground near us, but Trex spots him, too, and goes over to wake him.

"I'm fine, nothing I can't heal myself," I reply, slowly pulling up my sleeve to show my white rune.

"Good, get on with it. I'm going to wake Connor up, and find Nix. He can't be far," Trex tells me firmly. I don't argue with him, knowing I need to fix my arm to be able to fight and get us to the gate. I call my rune, feeling the power slam into my arm and slowly healing it. My wrist snaps back into place, and I bite back a scream.

"Blue, shit, I wish I had my rune powers to do

that for you," Connor says, hurriedly coming to my side. I give him a tight smile of appreciation as I finish healing my arm. Cutting off my power, I fall back on my butt, completely worn out as Connor offers me a hand once I get my breath back, and I get up, looking around. I can see the yellow light of the gate behind us, just beyond these rocks and the small stream of water that flows towards it.

"We need to follow the stream and get to the gate," I point at it with my newly mended arm, and Connor looks at where I'm pointing.

"I think we should dry off first and take a break," Connor replies, giving me a worried look like he thinks I need to rest like I'm a weak girl or something.

"No, I want to get to the next level. There have been way too many things looking and waiting for us on this level of Hell. I'm ready to leave," I tell him firmly.

"It's a good plan," Trex says from my right, and I frown at him as he walks over with Nix at his side.

"You're agreeing with me? Seriously?" I ask with a laugh that surprises even me.

"Don't count on it happening often, but this time, yes," he says as he crosses his arms. Nix pushes his hair off his face, revealing the long cut on his cheek that is still bleeding.

"Grab the bags and weapons. I'm going to heal Nix's face," I tell them, and they nod, doing as I ask. Nix smirks as I place my hand on his face, covering the cut.

"You just wanted to touch me again, didn't you?" Nix asks, and I shake my head.

"Shut up, and stay still," I mutter to him with a small smile, and call my white rune by simply closing my eyes this time. I don't need to touch it, I still have some of the power connected to me.

"I made you smile, that's enough for me, love," he states, and I open my eyes to see him staring down at me with a smile of his own. He has a really sexy smile, too, and the memory of his lips on mine makes me want to test kissing him again.

"Your cheek is healed," I say, clearing my throat and stepping back. I look over at Trex and Connor talking quietly and then over to the stream of water.

"We are ready," I say.

"What about the demon?" Trex asks.

"Azi will portal to the gate, he knows that's where we will be heading," I tell them, and walk ahead, knowing they will follow. I walk along the stream quietly for a while, drinking some of the water from my bag and eating another breakfast bar and some crisps from my bag. Unfortunately, only one bag of crisps survived the journey. The rest are too wet to eat. Trex catches up to me, walking by my side while the others stay behind us. I shoot him a questioning look.

"I'm sorry," Trex bites out, looking like it was difficult for him to say.

"What for?" I ask.

"For not listening to you and running out to those demons. It was stupid, and my mother taught me to say sorry for doing stupid shit. So, here I am," he admits with a shrug, and it's the first time that I don't find Trex to be a total asshole. *Colour me shocked.*

"Apology accepted. I expect you back to your dickhead self any time now," I say, making him laugh. He has one of those deep, sexy chuckles that could get any girl into bed, and I find that I want to hear it more.

"Sure."

"What are the princesses like, then? What's your fiancé like?" I ask, curious about who we are going after. Plus, I need to remind myself that he is going to be married.

"They are triplets, Emily, Esther, and my fiancé,

Erica," he explains, walking around a large rock as I go the other way, and we meet back on the other side. "Erica has black hair, blue eyes, and she is sweet . . . like her sisters are, too. That's why we have a trial coming up to decide a new queen. It's a fair way to choose a queen without just choosing the eldest like most do. Their mother died while we were under attack by demons, and our king died a few years later because of a great injury he got when he defended the children from another attack."

"So, there are no other royals?" I ask.

"They are all we have left of the royal family, and we need them. Every race has its strongest, and the royals are the strongest of our blood,"

"Wait, did you just describe your fiancé as 'sweet'?" I ask, taking in all of his history lesson. Of all the words I expected him to call his fiancé, sweet wasn't it. I notice how he talks about the royal family's past, rather than saying nice things about the woman he is meant to be in love with.

"Yes, 'sweet'," he replies, "Why, what's wrong with sweet?"

"I just didn't think sweet would be your type, that's all," I shrug.

"What do you think my type is then?" he asks.

"Not sweet, that's for sure," I say with a slight chuckle, and pause, seeing the gate and Azi a few feet in front of us. He walks over, and when he gets closer, I start to see that he doesn't look happy.

"What's wrong?" I ask, walking to his side.

"Come and see for yourself," he nods his head behind him, and I run up the little hill then abruptly stop.

"Crap," I mutter, seeing the massive gap in-between us and the gate on the other side. There is a rock in the middle, which I think I could jump to, and the wooden bridge is hanging down the side of it. There's a river underneath, and parts of the cliff are falling into it. Someone definitely doesn't want us following them to Hell, that's for sure.

"I found a bridge across, about three miles that way but I can't portal for a bit. I've used up too much energy," he points to the left as he explains. *Three miles? That will take ages.* "I'm going to tell the others," Azi says and walks over to Trex and Nix who are sitting near the stream, sifting through their bags. Connor comes to my side, and something in his eyes makes me think he knows I'm going to do something a little bit insane.

"Want to do something crazy?" I ask Connor, who frowns at me, as I keep an eye on the others.

"Like what?" he enquires.

"Jumping onto that rock, and then to the other side," I whisper, and he shakes his head. He's not quick enough to stop me as I run and jump, slamming into the edge of the rock, and using what's left of the wooden bridge to pull myself up.

"Now or never, Connor!" I shout, seeing Azi and the others looking around and spotting where I am. Connor shakes his head, stepping back for a running start before leaping at the last second. He lands pretty much in the same space I did. I grab his hand, pulling him up as the others get to the edge of the cliff and see what we have done. I ignore them and look over at the other side of the cliff, right by the gate.

"Don't you do it, Vi. I swear to the damn devil I will spank your ass if you do," Azi shouts at me from the other side. Ignoring him, I unclip my daggers from my belt and hold them at my sides. If anything, the idea of him trying to spank me just makes me want to jump more.

"Connor, fucking stop her!" Trex shouts from where he is standing next to Azi, and I look up at Connor. He is dripping with water like me, but it sticks to his leather outfit, making his gold hair stick around his face. His gold eyes are ablaze with mischief as he grins at me.

"Let's have some fun," I wink at him, and he laughs lifting his two daggers in the air and twirling them.

"Ladies first," he waves a hand towards the massive cliff that is crumbling before us, but it's the only way to get where we want to go quickly.

"I'm no lady," I laugh, but rush forward. I run fast towards the cliff and jump, lifting my hands gripping the daggers in the air and slamming them into the soft rock wall. I slide down a bit, but manage to save it. *Well, save myself.*

"You are both fucking crazy!" I hear Trex shout, just as Connor lands next to me.

"All the best people are! Good luck on the long way around boys!" I shout back and pull one of my daggers out, lifting it up, and slamming it into the soft rock above my head and continue like that, pulling myself up. *I think I like being crazy.*

Chapter Nineteen

EVIE

I WAVE ONCE MORE AT THE GUYS, SEEING THEIR annoyance, but fortunately not able to hear what they are shouting at us. Connor nods his head towards the gate, making me look away from the guys. The gate is literally a huge gold door that glows. There is a line of souls being led into it like they can't go anywhere else because it is said there a draw to this layer of hell for them. The souls that are not meant to be in Hell for long have to come here. They will be reborn, which is lucky for them. *I doubt my soul will be.*

"We can join the line. No one controls this gate, or protects it like the next one," I tell him. We walk the few steps to the line, slipping in between a gap and walking towards the door. The soul in front of me is an old lady in a long night dress, and her shiny hair is down. She looks so peaceful as she glides along, not even noticing me behind her.

"Who protects the next gate? Or do I not want to know?" Connor whispers as we walk.

"The three guard dogs of Hell. They aren't dogs, but they can turn themselves into massive creatures that look like dogs," I explain. I haven't met them myself, though. I only know what Azi has told me. He said they are immortal and bound to the gate, knowing they will die if they try to leave the gate unprotected. He also said they are assholes with appealing faces. And that the appeal was that he wanted to punch them every time they opened their mouths.

"How are we meant to get past them, exactly?" Connor asks, and I glance him expecting to see fear, but he just looks curious.

"Basically, by having Azi with us. They are forbidden from stopping him, along with anyone he wishes, from going into the third layer," I explain what I've heard. It's not like anyone asks to go down to hell, anyway, so I doubt the guard dogs will stop us.

"Why?" Connor asks.

"It's his home. Azi said he and his brothers were born there," I say quietly, and we finally get to the gate before Connor can ask any more questions. The soul in front of me walks straight into the gold wall like it's not there, disappearing on the other side. I step through, feeling as if a warm breeze hits me, and smile as I open my eyes to the second layer of Hell. It's a desert; the snow quickly changing to the open sands. There is a large pyramid in the center of this layer. The gold tip of the pyramid is shining in the sun. The vast distance between us and the pyramid clues me into the fact that's where the next portal is. I look around, seeing nothing else for ages. I know it's getting dark, and we need to find somewhere to hide before we try to make it to the next gate in the morning.

"This place is not what I was expecting," Connor says behind me, and he holds his hand over his eyes as he looks around.

"We need to find shelter for the night. It should be somewhere the others can find us," I say, and Connor puts his hand on my shoulder, turning me around.

"That looks good," he points at a small section of rocks. One of them is big enough to have a ledge that casts a shadow, and we can use it for a shelter for the night.

"Let's go," I say, walking over to the rocks. I keep an eye out, but there would only be demons here, and most will be near the pyramid. I doubt they will bother us. Souls can't be in here, they disappear once they go through the gate. We get to the rocks and I quickly look around to make sure we are safe before relaxing.

"The blue hair suits you, even wet," Connor randomly comments, making me turn to him.

"What is with you and my hair?"

"It just makes you so very beautiful," he tells me, making my heart pound. I don't reply, dropping my bags instead and pulling off my cloak and jacket. I'm left in just a vest shirt that is see through and my leggings. When I turn back to Connor, my mouth goes dry as I trace my eyes over his muscular, toned chest, and the rune name I can see written over his heart. I move my eyes up to his, and I see him staring at me with just as much desire as his eyes sweep down my body. I saunter over, watching him for any hesitance, but he doesn't move away, seemingly frozen to the spot. His rune name just looks like foreign symbols to me, all different marks that make no sense. I place my hand on his chest and lightly begin tracing them with my finger, making his breath hitch.

"I should push you away," he whispers as I lock my eyes with his. I smirk, tilting my head up, so our lips are inches apart.

"You *should*, but you won't. It will feel so much better because you know it's not allowed," I tease him, brushing my lips against his. He loses control quickly, grabbing my hips and pulling me into his arms as he harshly kisses me. I didn't expect his kiss to be quite like this. Demanding, harsh, controlling, and utterly amazing. It's always the quiet ones you should watch out for. He walks us backward, pushing my back against the rock wall, and only breaking away from my lips to kiss down my neck. I open my eyes for only a second and see red ones glaring at me from a few feet away. I don't stop Connor as he sucks on my neck, in fact, I urge him on a bit. Azi's eyes glow as he storms towards us, and then he grabs Connor, sending him flying away from me into the sand.

"You. Are. Mine!" Azi growls possessively, stepping into my space and grabbing my arms, pinning them above my head. I could fight him off, but I don't when I realise how close he is to losing control.

"Like fuck I am! You're a cheating bastard!" I seethe, not scared of him one bit.

"You never let me explain! You just walked away, you left!" he growls right back.

"I don't need an explanation, I know what I saw!" I shout back.

"You don't know fuck. The woman you walked into the room and saw between my legs was sent as a present from my brother. I didn't even know she was in my apartment when I walked in and sat down. She practically ran to me as the door was unlocked, and from there, everything happened so fast," he tells me, and I don't breathe as I think it through. Could that have happened? I was so angry, so upset that I didn't give him or her a chance to say anything to me before I called a portal to Hell. "You know what I think? You wanted a reason to run . . . you can't handle the chance that someone is actually on your side. That someone cares about you, and that you're not alone anymore."

"You really expect me to believe that?" I eventually say, but my voice comes out in a hoarse whisper because I don't want to admit that I might have been wrong. And I *hate* just how accurate he probably is in his assessment of me. I do run from anyone that gets too close to me. They usually leave or die anyway. I've had twenty-five years of experience with people doing that, starting off with my parents who left me. I keep my eyes locked on his, filled with more emotion than I ever wanted to show this demon.

"I have never lied to you. *Never*, Vi," he says firmly before he finally lets me go, stepping away as Connor runs over to us. I spot Trex and Nix walking over the sand hill in the distance, and I know I need to focus on the mission. I have to get the princesses back, so Hali is safe. Nothing else matters.

"I can't deal with this, not here and not now. I can only think of Hali; she needs me," I tell him, trying to clear my head of everything going on between us for now. I hate the fact he can scare me so easily by being truthful.

"I know, that's why I'm not pressing you . . . but don't push me," he warns.

"Everything okay, Evie?" Connor asks as he moves closer, wiping sand out of his hair and keeping his eyes on Azi the whole time.

"Yeah, everything is fine. Azi got the stupid notion that I belong to him somehow, when I don't. I don't belong to anyone, and I can do as I damn well please," I say forcefully, moving away from them all and going to my bag. I look over my shoulder once at Azi, seeing him and Connor watching me as they talk quietly. I shake my head as I look back at my bag. I can't trust him, I can't believe him, and I can't risk thinking about my ex while I'm literally in Hell.

Chapter Twenty

EVIE

"I SEE SOMETHING, EVERYONE GET UP!" NIX SAYS, from his position as lookout at the front of the rock. I sit up quickly, grabbing a dagger and running to his side. I look to where he is pointing and blow out a sigh of relief as I hold my hand up to pause the others.

"They are traders, nothing that will bother us," I say loud enough that the others can hear me. Traders are demons who literally do what their name suggests, they trade. A few years back, a bunch of them decided to try kidnapping humans and trading them to demons here as a new business venture. They were all killed by Protectors, who even had the help of some demons who thought they had gone too far. I'm surprised to even see any trader demons alive anymore. These traders must have hidden when everyone went after them. They look like they are trading junk, though, and a lot of it. I look at them when they get closer, noticing they are not good-looking demons at all. They have green skin covered in bumps, with large round stomachs, beady eyes, and long green cloaks on. There are two of them pulling, what looks like, a couple of stolen supermarket trollies behind them that are overflowing with junk. *How they are even getting those carts to move in that sand is beyond me.*

"Why are they coming this way?" Trex asks from just behind me, and I shrug.

"They will try to trade you things, it's what they do. They didn't always trade humans. That was just a few of their kind that were evil, and they were all killed because of the actions of a few. I'm sure you killed many of their families," I say, patting his arm as I walk past. He glares at me, not liking the truth. "They are harmless and still people–don't kill them or I'll have to kill you myself."

"Fine," Trex growls, going back to the rock, as I put my dagger back in my belt and go to my bag. Digging through my bag, I decide to take stock of my supplies. I have four breakfast bars, three protein bars, and some other random snacks left. I only have two bottles of water, which isn't the best reserve when we have a hot desert to cross, but it will have to do.

"I miss bacon already and real meals," I groan, shoving everything back the bag and doing it up. At least my bag is lighter now, and I don't have to carry any arrows. I lost them all in the river, along with my bow. At least I still have my daggers, it's something.

"I have bacon rasher crisps. I don't usually share them, but you look desperate," Connor says, opening his bag, and going through it as I move to his side. He pulls out the small packet of crisps and hands them to me. I smile as I take them, flashing back to memories of stealing them from shops as a kid.

"I used to steal these as kid. There was this little corner shop just outside the demon underground. When I was starving, and my friend couldn't get me food, these were the easiest and cheapest thing to steal," I tell Connor, though I don't really know why I even told him. "I guess it's why I became obsessed with bacon."

"I'm sorry you had a life like that," he says.

"Don't be. I had a friend who was like a sister to me, and a roof over my head. There were demon and human children in far worse places than I was," I say, knowing from some of the things I saw, I was one of the lucky ones. Kids typically don't last long on the streets without being sold or killed. I was so lucky to have a guardian, in a way.

"Who was your friend?" he asks.

"Hali's mum, and she died what seems like a long time ago," I tell him, looking away as he places his hand on my arm.

"She would be proud of you for protecting her daughter. Maybe one day, you can tell me about her? I would like to know more about her and you," he says, moving his hand away, not pushing me into an answer.

"Maybe. Anyway, thanks for these," I say, practically inhaling the crisps the moment I open them. I look over to see Azi leaning against the wall, still glaring at me like he has been all night. Quickly glancing away, I notice Nix talking to the traders. I watch as he holds his hands up in the air, shaking his head, and I realise that they might not speak English, and he could probably use my help.

"I'm going to check on Nix," I tell Connor, standing up, and putting the empty wrapper in my trouser pocket. Connor looks over at Nix and nods at me.

"I don't understand you," Nix is saying when I get closer, and the demons stop talking to him to look at me instead.

"Artis? Artis?" The demon on the right repeats over and over. His eyes straying to the daggers on Nix's belt.

"Non artis. Vos should relinquere," I tell them, explaining that we don't want to trade. The one on the right nods, huffing, and walks away with his friend following.

"Hearing you speak Latin is kinda sexy, love," Nix whispers as the traders turn around, and start walking away slowly. I hear a little meow, and then I spot the cage in the back of their trolley underneath some metal rubbish.

"Is that a tiger?" Nix asks, leaning forward to look.

"Yeah, and only a baby by the looks of it. Shame it's down here. Animals like that need to be on Earth and not trapped in Hell," I say, feeling sorry for it, but there is nothing we can do. Nix looks at me, smiling widely, and then back at the traders.

"Could we trade for it?" Nix asks, and before I can stop him, he shouts for the traders to come back. "I'm going to trade for it."

"What the hell are we going to do with a small tiger where we are going? Other than hope it doesn't bite us?" I harshly whisper at Nix, who shrugs, pulling a gold dagger from his belt. The trader's eyes widen when they see the dagger, practically drooling with excitement.

"The tiger for the dagger," Nix holds it up, showing them what he means without having to speak Latin. The traders nod happily, watching Nix walk around them, and lift the small metal cage out from beneath the rubbish. The tiger is a baby like we thought, about the size of a small child, and the cage is too small for her or him as it's squished inside. It has white fur and black lines around the fur on its face are the only pattern I can see. It's cute, I'll admit that, but this is still a bad idea. We are going to have a fight on our hands and we are trying to rescue three princesses from the depths of Hell. I guess three princesses and a tiger now. *That sounds like a fairy tale waiting to be written.* The traders quickly snatch the dagger from Nix when he gets back, and one licks it before putting it in his cloak and walking away. *Gross.* Connor and Azi walk over, looking at the tiger in the cage, and Connor groans.

"You bought a tiger. Are you fucking serious?" Connor asks.

"Another thing to protect, good job," Azi sarcastically comments, but Nix doesn't care, or even bother replying to them. I look back at the rocks to see Trex sitting on them, watching us, and he doesn't appear impressed. I almost want to shout that I had nothing to do with this, just so I don't have to hear his lecture. He is definitely going to have a lecture waiting.

"Let's get you out, little girl," Nix coos and puts the cage on the floor, opening the locked door.

"Girl? How do you know?" Connor asks as we watch the tiger come out of the cage, stepping on the sand cautiously and watching us all.

"Just a guess, but she is too pretty to be a boy," Nix shrugs. The tiger is looking directly at me as Nix talks, and suddenly, she starts to run towards me. At the last second, she jumps, landing straight in my arms. She immediately starts licking my face. When I pull away she starts to whine, so I hold her close again.

"She likes you," Connor chuckles as I try to get the tiger to stop licking my chin.

"Can you blame her?" Nix grins, and I roll my eyes at him as I look down at her as she begins to settle down. . I notice she has a collar on when she turns her head to lie on my arm, and I spin it around until I see the tag.

"She must have had an owner, she has a tag. Her name is Star, apparently," I tell them, and they all step closer to inspect the tag. There isn't anything else on it, other than the name. The collar looks expensive though, with silver stars embedded into the black leather.

"Maybe I should catch up to them and find out where they stole her from," I say, looking around, but I can't see the traders anymore; they are long gone. "Or maybe not."

"They are likely dead, which means you will have to look after her," Nix says, folding his arms. "Think of it as a present."

"Er, nope. I don't do pets, or cute animal side-kicks like heroes have in movies. I'm not the hero here, buddy," I say, making them all chuckle as I scowl at them. I try to put Star in Nix's arms, but she cries, crawling on my chest and scratching me.

"Alright! Fine!" I say, glaring at the stupidly cute animal, and walking back to the rocks. Trex just raises his eyebrows at me.

"Don't say a word. Not one word," I warn him, opening my bag and looking down at Star.

"I will carry you, but you have to go in the bag

in case I need to fight. Do you understand?" I ask, and then realise I'm talking to a tiger who can't answer me. I'm surprised when she doesn't fight me as I place her in my bag and do up the sides a little bit to hold her in. She puts her paws out, tilting her head as she looks up at me with a happy expression. I don't know how to explain that I know she is happy, she just looks it. I would let her walk, but the sand is deep, and we don't have any kind of lead.

"Here," Trex kneels down next to me, offering Star a stick of jerky. She jumps and snatches it out of his hand, lying down in the bag to chew it.

"Thanks," I say, for Star. "Didn't know you had a kind side."

"I wouldn't want her to starve, that's all," he grumbles at me and stands up, walking away to grab his bag. I lift my bag on my back, trying not to swear at how heavy Star makes it now.

"Let's go," I say, walking straight towards the pyramids, with a purring, cute tiger as a new friend.

Chapter Twenty-One

EVIE

"WHY DO DEMONS END UP WITH SO MANY BLONDES in Hell?" Connor asks, and I raise my eyebrows at him.

"Not another bad joke. You really aren't going to make me laugh by telling me these. Hasn't the last half an hour taught you anything?" I say, and he laughs.

"Nope. And the answer is . . . because they're so hot! Get it," he knocks my shoulder, and I just shake my head at him. "Okay, okay. What do I need to do to make you laugh, then?" he asks me.

"Nothing, I don't know," I mutter.

"I will find a joke that makes you laugh one day, Blue," he grins, and it makes me smile. No, he won't, but I'm not going to burst his bubble. I look ahead as we walk over a sand dune, seeing the entrance to the pyramid. There are demons everywhere, walking around the small market outside the entrance. We will have to keep our heads down to get through them, and hope no one important notices us. I hold my hand up, waiting for the others to catch up to me. They all stop, sliding their bags off, and getting out their water for a drink. I do the same, reaching around Star who is sleeping in the bag, snoring loudly. I gave her some water an hour ago, so I know she is alright. *Cute little tiger.* I drink my water, pouring some on my face to wash the sweat away, before speaking.

"We are getting close, and we can expect there will be something waiting for us. Whoever took your princesses must know we killed and escaped their traps by now. Demons talk," I tell them. Trex picks his axe up, holding it on his shoulder.

"We will be ready," he says.

"Everyone be alert, and keep your heads down. None of us look like demons, other than red eyes over here," I point a finger at Azi.

"I will walk ahead," Azi says and walks off before we can agree with him. I catch up, walking just behind him as we go down the sand dune and towards the stone path where there are a few demons dotted around.

"How much do you trust these Protectors?" Azi asks me quietly, never turning to look at me as he speaks.

"Not at all," I answer simply. They could betray me at any second.

"I could take you out of here, and we could get Hali back together," he whispers. I look back at Connor, who is a few steps behind me, and then at Trex and Nix.

"It wouldn't work. Trust me, I have thought about killing them and getting out of here, but that risks Hali's life. I can't do that," I whisper back. We walk past a few demons talking quietly, their eyes watch us with curiosity, but they don't move.

"I don't like this. I feel like I'm missing something," Azi says.

"Same. Can you do something for me?" I ask, and he looks back at me for a brief second, nodding.

"Anything for you, Vi," he replies in a warm and affectionate tone.

"If anything happens, portal and find Hali. Keep her safe, she is everything. Okay?"

"For you, I promise. Nothing will happen to

you, though," he says darkly, and I believe him. I know he would do anything to save me, and if I'm honest with myself, I don't think I would let him die either. I move back next to Connor, letting Azi lead the way.

"I have a question," Trex says in a demanding tone, sliding into the gap between me and Connor.

"What?" I ask.

"How do we get out of the third layer of Hell when we get the princesses back?" he asks. "The way we came, it's too dangerous to take them back that way." I keep my head down as we enter the market. It's full of more demons than I thought. My hair covers my face well, anyway, but there is too much chance of someone here recognising me.

"There is a way," Azi answers, looking back. "I will not tell you how. It is a family secret. You will just have to trust me." He speaks with a creepy grin that no one in their right mind would trust.

"Guess I'll have to, demon," he says. *Well, clearly Trex is crazy.*

"Everyone gather around! Gather around! We have a new sale!" I hear someone shout, and I look around to see where its coming from. We keep walking and see the demon standing on top of a row of cages. Demons are all gathered around them, so I can't see what is in the cages from here.

"Auctions are banned, what are they selling?" I ask Azi.

"Leave it. It doesn't have anything to do with us, and we can't draw trouble to ourselves," Azi warns me, giving me a look that tells me I should do as he says. Purely because of that look, I slip away from him and into the crowd. I hear him shout my name from behind as I pull myself through the crowd of demons and get to the front. Everything seems to go silent as I look at the demon children in the cages. They have rags on skinny frames, and most are hidden in the corners, scared. One cage is full of women, all stunning demons, but they don't look in the best condition.

"What the fuck?" I mutter, looking up the demon who is selling them, shouting prices into the crowd with a greedy look on his ugly face. He is greasy, that's literally the only way to describe him. He has red skin, spikes on his head that go down his arm, and expensive clothes on. I move my hand to my dagger, but Azi gets to my side, placing his hand over mine.

"No. You do this, and we have to kill all of his

bodyguards. Likely most of this crowd as well, and if we die, no one protects Hali," he warns me.

"If I do nothing, I will never forgive myself. I was a child, just like them, and left alone with no one to protect me. Hali's mother was the only one that did the right thing, and that's what she taught me to do. The. Right. Thing," I tell him, knocking his hand away and sliding my dagger out.

"Then we are with you," I hear Connor say from behind me. Trex gets his axe out, nodding at me, and Nix grins as he unclips his daggers. I look up at Azi, who shakes his head, but slowly removes his sword from its sheath.

"Make your move, Vi. I'm here," he says. I grin, lifting my dagger over my shoulder as I step in front of the crowd and fling it straight into the neck of the seller. His eyes widen as his gasps fill the air, and then screams from the crowd immediately follow, as the five demon bodyguards run at us. I head straight for the biggest one in the middle, seeing how slow he is moving. He narrows his eyes at me as he lifts a purple sword into the air. *I like that sword.* I spin to the left at the last second and slice his sword carrying arm with my dagger. He growls, switching the sword to his other hand and running at me again. I wait this time, allowing him to get close enough to swing the sword straight at my head. I quickly shift backwards, making him stumble past me on my right, and I spin around, throwing my dagger straight into his back. Right where his heart is. The bodyguard screams, falling to the floor and dropping the sword. I look around to see Azi has already killed two of the bodyguards, and the Protectors only have two left to kill. *They can handle it.* All the demons from the crowd have fled, clearly not wanting to be part of any hassle. *Cowards.* I walk over, pulling my dagger out of his now dead body, and wipe the blood on his top before putting it back. I pick the sword up, looking it over. The whole blade is made of a purple metal, with silver tips, and it shines. There are symbols all down the one side. *I'm keeping this.*

"Nice," Connor comments with a whistle, getting to my side and looking down at the sword.

"It is," I reply, sliding my old sword out of the holder on my back, and putting the new one in. My old sword was just silver, nothing special. "It's mine now." I grin at him. I run, jumping on the cage and climbing up, pulling myself to the top. I kick the body of the seller over and grab the five keys off his belt. I climb back down, holding the keys out.

"Here, help me unlock the cages," I hand the

RUNES OF TRUTH

guys a key each. Luckily the cages and keys have numbers on them, making it easy to unlock them. I go to mine, number one, and unlock the door. The child looks up, shaking her head of red hair with scared eyes.

"You're free, do you understand?" I ask, and she nods, standing up. I flinch at the small bruises on her shoulders that are visible and wish I had made the seller's death longer, more painful. "Come on, kid." I nod my head at the door and hold my hand out. I don't expect her to take my hand as she walks forward, but she does. Her cold hand slides into mine. Demons usually run hotter than normal, and yet, she feels freezing.

"Let's find someone to look after you," I tell her, and she smiles up at me.

"Salvator," she whispers. *Saviour.*

Chapter Twenty-Two

EVIE

"The women won't come out, they are too frightened," Nix says as I walk to his side, looking in the cage where he has opened the door. The women are huddled together in the corner, none of them looking our way as they cower and hide. I glance over to the other cages, seeing Trex and Connor walking three little children over to us. Trex is even making one of them smile, and it's not what I expected at all. *Who knew he had a soft spot for kids?* Azi is kneeling down in one of the cages, talking slowly to a little boy who doesn't seem to want to move.

"They likely don't speak English," I comment, glancing back at the women just as one of the them looks up, and she stands up slowly. The woman's long, red hair is dirty and is barely held back in a ponytail. There is dirt all over her face, but it doesn't take away from the strength in her green eyes or her tight-lipped expression. Her eyes widen when she looks at me, and then over to my side.

"Karaisa?" the woman asks, looking at the little girl who is still holding my hand. She lets go, running to the woman who grabs her, and holds her tight. Her eyes full of tears meet mine, standing up, and holding the little girl.

"I speak English. At least some," she says slowly, though she's clearly struggling to think of the correct words. I start to speak to her in Latin, but decide that Nix might want to hear what she has to say. He helped save them, after all.

"Is she your daughter?" Nix asks, and she nods, giving him a fearful look. They are all obviously scared of men, and I feel sorry for them. Hopefully in time, they will forget being here.

"It's okay, we mean you no harm. You are free, all of you," I say firmly, and she gives us a confused look as Connor, Azi, and Trex walk towards us. The children run into the cage, and the women grab them when they are near, crying as they hold tight to their children. "Free," I repeat firmly.

"Thank you. Can I have your name?" she asks.

"Salvator," Karaisa pipes up before I can answer, and her mum nods, repeating the name louder. All the women and children repeat it, as they stand and walk out of the cage, each one bowing their heads at me. Karaisa and her mum are the last ones to come out, and she stops right in front of me.

"We return to our husbands. We never forget, Salvator," she tells me, and walks away. I look at my old sword on the ground, and I make a split-second decision. Quickly grabbing the sword, I run after the slaves. Karaisa pulls her mum's hair when she sees me, and her mum turns around, giving me a confused look.

"This is yours. It will keep you safe, or you can use it to trade," I say, pushing the sword into her spare hand.

"We never forget," she says, and I know it's her way of saying thank you. I watch her turn and walk away until she has disappeared into the market of people that eye us warily.

"Do you think they will be safe?" Connor asks, as he gets to my side. The others come over as well, and I look up at Connor.

"I hope so, but at least we gave them a chance.

Everyone deserves a chance," I say, and he places his hand on my arm for only a second.

"You're right," he whispers and steps away.

"Time to go. I don't want to be on this level of Hell when it gets dark," Trex tells us as he walks ahead, and we have no choice but to follow.

"Azi, you should go in front," I say to him when he stays near my side.

"I know," is all he replies, but he stays right next to me. Nix and Connor walk behind us, and I keep flashing my eyes back to them, remembering how I've kissed them both, and we have been interrupted each time. I would like to not be interrupted at some point.

"You like them, the Protectors," Azi comments, and I look back at him, feigning ignorance.

"I don't have a clue—"

"I like it," he interrupts me, and I laugh.

"Seriously? Sharing was not something I had you down for," I say, still chuckling as his red eyes stare down at me. "Not that sharing is even an option for us, considering we aren't together."

"We will be together again, but I think you will be with them also. I see the way you look at them, and how they look at you. At first, I wanted to cut their dicks off, but now, I believe they are good for you," he says, his eyes watching my own as I look up at him. I don't even want to touch the subject of him arrogantly thinking we will be back together.

"Why do you think they are good for me?" I ask, curious.

"They bring out this side to you, a different side than the defensive Vi I've always known. You never let me in, not ever, even if you tell yourself that you did. There has always been this wall, and I think you need more than one person to knock it down," he says.

"I didn't put a wall up with you, I gave you what I could," I argue, but it's a weak argument, and we both know it.

"You can't even see the wall because it's been there since you were a baby. You don't know how to trust, how to fully love. Life for you has always been a fight, a struggle, and you never had someone fully at your side that you could trust," he says, and I look away.

"I don't want to talk about this anymore," I say, stepping in front of him, and he doesn't stop me. We walk in silence up to the entrance of the pyramid, and Azi finally steps in front of us as we pass through the open stone door. The pyramid is empty inside, with sand floors and one spiral staircase that goes all the way up to the top. At the top is a gold light, but it's so bright that I can't see anything else up there.

"The only way is up," Azi says, walking to the staircase and starts climbing. I jog to catch up, and the others follow as we walk up the dusty, sand-covered steps. The steps are huge, causing me to have to lift my legs up high to make each step.

"What were these steps built for? Giants?" I mutter, making Azi laugh.

"No, there used to be a royal family of Hell, and it is said the very first queen of Hell was a goddess. There are no royals around to tell us if that was true or not, though," Azi tells us. *Royals of Hell? Sounds like a terrible inheritance.* It takes ages to climb all the steps to the top, and I'm out of breath by the time we get to the clearing.

"You should do more cardio, you clearly need it," Trex comments.

"You need the stick that is stuck up your ass removed, but you don't hear me offering you advice," I reply as Trex glares down at me, going to step closer.

"Enough," Azi snaps, making me look away from Trex, to see him waving a fire-covered hand over what looked like an empty circular space. The ward, or whatever it is, burns away with Azi's touch, and a bigger room appears. This one isn't empty. No, it has five doors and polished stone floors with fire in pots around the room. Four of the doors are wooden, nothing special about them, and the one in the middle looks like it's made of solid glass. You can't see anything other than smoke through it, and if I had to guess what a door to heaven would look like, this would be it, not the door to the deepest level of Hell.

"Azi, my man, what do we have here?"

Chapter Twenty-Three

EVIE

I FOLLOW THE DEEP VOICE OF THE MAN THAT SPOKE to see the door to the far right is open, and a demon is leaning on the door frame. He only has jeans on, with a cheeky grin on his attractive face, and a mop of messy red hair. His black eyes look at us all, before settling on me.

"Azi, tut, tut, tut. You shouldn't bring a beauty such as her to place like this," he comments as he ambles over to me, but Azi places his hand on his chest, stopping him from coming too close.

"Touch her, and I will enjoy killing you, Cody," Azi warns, and Cody laughs, pushing his hand away and walking over to the other doors. He bangs on them both, before leaning on the wall in the middle of them.

"Who have you let into Hell recently? And were there three women with them?" Trex asks, stepping next to Azi. Cody's eyes go to Azi, who nods, and then back to Trex.

"I will tell you what you want . . . for a price," he replies as the door on his right is opened, and a demon who looks the mirror image of Cody steps out, narrowing his eyes on Azi.

"The wayward overlord returns," he looks at us, "with friends, it seems."

"It's none of your business, Caleb," Azi snaps.

"You're right, it's not. You and your brothers are playing with fire, and every single one of you will be burned for it," Caleb replies dryly.

"What does that mean?" Azi demands, and Caleb looks at Cody rather than answering.

"Have my key and let them in, I want no part in this," he says as he pulls a necklace off and hands it to Cody before striding back to the door he came out of and slamming it behind him.

"Sorry about that, my brother is a dick," Cody explains.

"At least you know it. Let's hope he realises it sometime soon," I say, and Cody laughs, standing up.

"So, a price for the information? You want to make a deal, man?" Cody asks Trex, who looks at the smoky door, and then back to Cody.

"Yes."

"I will tell you some shit you are sure to find interesting, if you promise to do anything I ask when I call on you. I'm not crazy, so it won't be killing anyone, or any shit like that, but that is my offer," Cody says, but I wouldn't trust him. He smiles like the creepy Cheshire cat from Alice in Wonderland when Trex offers his hand to shake on the deal, and Cody shakes it.

"Done. I will keep my promise," Trex assures him.

"Oh, I know you will. You seem like one of those serious fucks that keep your promises," Cody grins.

"What do you know? We don't have all day," Nix interjects.

"About a week ago, one of his brothers came through here with three women. All of them were tied up and had bags on their heads, so I couldn't see their faces," he tells us, and I watch as Trex tightens his hands into fists and looks back at Connor and Nix.

"Which brother?" Azi asks, and the seriousness on his face makes me a little concerned for a second.

"Roth," Cody says quietly.

"Shit," Azi replies, rubbing his face. "Cody, go find your other brother, and give us a minute alone."

"Sure, no thanks for the advice or anything," Cody grumbles, but walks over to the door he knocked on that no one came out of and opens it up, stepping inside and slamming it shut behind him.

"Is Roth someone we should worry about?" Connor asks exactly what I was wondering.

"I was hoping this had nothing to do with any of my brothers, but it looks like it does," Azi admits, not looking happy about it.

"Why would your brother steal the princesses?" Nix asks.

"Roth has a thing for science, and it's not a good thing. He likes to create creatures, mix bloods, and in general mess with nature. When I saw those green creatures that came after us, I wondered if Roth could have sent them," Azi admits. "His sin is curiosity."

"Didn't your brother ever hear the human saying 'curiosity killed the cat'? Because that would be a good lesson for him," I remark, but they all ignore me.

"Then your brother has to die," Trex coldly remarks.

"I can deal with one of my brothers at a time, and *possibly* kill him. That's only if Roth hasn't gotten the help of any of my other brothers."

"We need to get to them quickly then, if your brother is going to be doing weird tests on them or something,"

"Yes, we do," Trex answers, and the door Cody left through opens at the end of his words. Cody walks out first followed by his brother. His brother looks just like a slightly older version of Cody. He has a full red-haired beard that matches his trimmed hair, and black eyes that watch us all for a brief second.

"You want entry? You sure?" the bearded man asks in a deep voice.

"Yes," Azi says simply, no need for messing around.

"Let's get this out of the way, then," Cody says, clapping his hands together and stepping up to the door. I watch as he gets the necklace his brother gave him out of his pocket and places the triangular, metal symbol in a space on the door for it. It glows red as Cody's brother pulls a bracelet off his wrist, with a metal circle symbol in another gap and it glows red, too. Cody finally pulls a ring off his finger, and it has a square symbol on it. The moment it touches the space where Cody places it, it too glows red.

"Patentibus," Cody almost growls out and presses his hand to the door. The glass just melts away into smoke, though the smoke still holds the shape of the door. Cody steps back, waving a hand at the door.

"Time to go," he says and looks over at me, trailing his eyes over my body slowly. "Though, *you* are always welcome back." Azi whacks Cody on the head as he passes him and walks into the smoky door.

"Ouch, dickhead! That's not how you say thank you!" Cody shouts as Trex and Nix follow after Azi. Connor just waits, crossing his arms.

"I'm not leaving him alone with you. Go on," Connor states. Cody laughs, "Smart man."

"Later, boys," I say, walking forward and stepping into the smoky door. The smoke smothers me for a few seconds, making me cough before the third layer of Hell appears.

"Watch out!" Trex shouts, just as a dagger comes flying through the air towards me.

Chapter Twenty-Four

EVIE

I FALL TO THE GROUND, WATCHING THE DAGGER fly over my head, and disappear into the smoky door behind me. *I hope Connor is okay.* I quickly jump up and look around, seeing Azi holding a demon in the air by his neck, and there isn't anyone else around. The dagger distracted me for a second, but now I can't help but look around. It is beautiful. There are fields and fields of green grass, and trees with large red apples hanging from them for as far as you can see. I spot a building in the far distance, and I can hear the sound of running water in the distance, too. This place reminds me of the Garden of Eden that I read about as a kid. Where the first humans were said to have come from. I look up at the sky, seeing thousands of stars, which is impossible because there can't be stars down here. There are so many that it's bright enough to look like it's day.

"Who threw the dagger? It missed me by an inch!" Connor exclaims as he comes through the portal, holding the dagger up in his hand.

"He did," Trex points at the man Azi is holding in the air. The man, well demon, has red skin and hair, and leather clothes. His cloak is on the floor, as are a range of weapons that Azi has clearly taken off him.

"Why did you wait for Evie?" Azi demands, shaking the demon as we all walk over.

"Sent. Kill," the demon coughs out. Azi grabs his head, snapping his neck, and lets the demon's body drop to the ground before anyone can ask anything else.

"I don't get why he waited for you," Azi growls.

"If you hadn't kill him straight away, we might have been able to find out," Connor replies sarcastically.

"He wouldn't have talked. I could tell," Azi shrugs.

"The demon clearly knew to take out the deadliest opponent first," I say, and each one of them turns to glare at me.

"That is not the reason," Nix states firmly, and the others nod.

"It is, and you all know it," I say with a wide smile, leaning down and taking off my bag. "We might as well have a food break. It looks safe enough here, and you've already killed the obvious danger." I don't wait for the guys to agree or not before putting my bag down, and grinning at Star, who is still sleeping in the bag.

"You like to sleep a lot, huh?" I ask, and she yawns as I pick her up and take her out of the bag. I pull my last water bottle out, drinking half and then pouring the other half in the small box I kept my food in. She happily drinks away as Azi comes over, kneeling down next to us. Star watches him, almost narrowing her eyes at him, until I stroke her back, and she goes back to drinking her water.

"You like her, so I like her," he tells me as he places a small box full of broken up jerky and what looks like bacon rasher crisps. "It's all we have that she might eat, but we can get real food when we are out of Hell." I look over to see the others watching, but they all quickly look away when I see them, making me smile.

"Thanks," I tell Azi, and he smiles at me before going back over to his bag.

"Spoilt already," I say to Star, stroking her head, and sitting down next to her. I pull out what is left of my food and start to eat, watching the Protectors and Azi. They all sit near me, occasionally looking in my direction. I have the feeling they are protecting me, when I don't need it. I finish off my food, waiting for Star to finish hers before putting everything back in the bag as Star goes off for the toilet. I copy her idea, walking to a nearby tree and relieving myself. I walk back to the guys to see Star on Connor's lap, and he is doing something to her collar.

"What are you doing?" I ask, stroking Star's head when she nudges my hand. *Fussy tiger.*

"I found rope in the demon's stuff, so I made a lead. It will be good for her to stretch her legs," Connor says, lifting the thin rope he has tied to her collar and handing me the handle loop he has tied.

"Thanks, I'm sure Star will appreciate it," I say, walking away a little and encouraging Star to follow by gently pulling the rope. She jumps off Connor's lap, after licking his face first, and wanders over to my side.

"How are there stars here?" I ask Azi as he tightens the straps on his bag and walks next to my side. Trex walks with Nix just behind us, and

Connor catches up, coming straight to my side with Star in-between us.

"They aren't stars," he says.

"I've heard a rumour that the lights down here are the souls of angels," Connor says, his words seeming to echo around us.

"Everyone knows angels don't exist anymore," I say, remembering the story Hali's mum told me once. Humans didn't always know demons or any supernaturals existed until an angel fell from heaven. Not just one angel, but five. The angels were evil and started killing everything they could find, so the supernaturals and demons stood in front of the humans and defended them. Working together, they killed the angels, but thousands lost their lives. Angels were more powerful than anything. The laws for supernaturals and demons were introduced, and the Protectors were the ones made to enforce those laws.

"My oldest brother told me something once about the stars, and he is so old that it could possibly be true," Azi says.

"Tell us then, Az," I nudge his shoulder, and he looks up at the stars for a second.

"He said that once this place and heaven were so very close together, that angels would come and spend many of their days living with demons. It all changed one day when an angel killed a demon, and a war erupted between them. Thousands of angels and demons were killed right where we stand. The stars were said to appear when an angel died here, and the darkness was the demons who were lost. My brother swore the sky was nothing other than blue before the war," he says, almost sadly.

"That's a beautiful story," I say, looking up at the stars or lights. Or angels' souls. Whatever they are, they are stunning.

"My brother died shortly after telling me that because he lost his mind. He pretty much brought me up, and these stars remind me of him when he wasn't evil," he tells us, and I look over, getting lost in his eyes for a second. You would think the redness of his eyes, the unnatural glow they always have, and the depth of them would be scary, but I can't look away. His eyes are so different, and they suit him. They *are* him.

"Where are we heading, then?" Connor asks, snapping me out of it. Azi lifts his hand, pointing at the white building in the far distance, right in the middle of a big open grass field.

"There. My old home."

Chapter Twenty-Five

EVIE

WE TREK ACROSS THE EMPTY FIELD, ANXIOUS AND alert. Star is back in my bag, and both of my daggers are in my hands. I don't trust the quiet and stillness of this place, or the lack of guards surrounding the lands. There should have been someone here to stop us. I glance at Trex, who has both of his axes in his hands, and his eyes roam around us every few seconds. He doesn't trust this, either. The house gradually comes into view, and it's less of a house and more of a stadium you'd expect to find in Greece. It's completely white, with dozens of pillars on the walls outside, and only one large door as an entrance.

"This is too easy," I say quietly. "Nothing should be this simple here."

"I know." That's all Azi replies to me, and the others are silent. Connor looks over at me, pulling his sword out, and stepping closer. I look to my right to see Nix has done the same thing as Connor; all of us are on high alert now. We walk faster up to the door, and Azi walks in first, with us all following him inside the dusty room.

"What is that smell?" I ask, holding my hand over my nose at the overwhelming smell of rot that fills the room.

"I have a torch, one sec," I hear Connor say, and hear him rifling around in his bag.

"I'm sorry," I hear Azi say, the regret and compassion clear in his voice. Connor flashes the light on, and the sight of two bodies on the floor greet us. Connor's flashlight falls to the floor, and I hear him stagger back, but I don't take my eyes off the dead women.

"No," Nix rasps out, his voice full of grief and horror. Azi throws a ball of fire up to the ceiling, lighting up the entire room after a brief silence. The women both have black hair, pretty faces, and long black cloaks on that cover all of their body except their faces and arms. Their arms are spread wide and burnt, but you can still see where their runes used to be. They stare up at the ceiling with dead, empty eyes. I know straight away that they are the princesses from the reactions I see on the Protectors' faces when I finally turn to look at them. I stand still as Connor walks to the side of one of the women, kneeling down, and closing her eyes with his fingers. Trex walks to the other woman's side, doing the same, and unclipping his cloak. He covers her face and bows his head, whispering some words. Connor covers the other woman as I look around at the wall, seeing the writing in blood on the wall.

"Come to me. The last one is where the sun touches Hell," I read out loud. I feel Azi come to my side, looking at the message with me.

"I know where that is, it's not far from here. We should go if we are to have a chance of saving the last princess," he says, and Trex looks at us as we turn around.

"No. We bury Emily and Esther. We can't take their bodies with us, but I will not leave them here in Hell like this. We will have a fire built," Trex demands, his angry eyes trained on me. I don't think he is angry at me, but he will direct his ire at us if we refuse. I can tell he needs to bury them before doing anything else.

"That could take all day and well into the night, and the last—" Azi starts off.

"He will keep her alive. Roth is playing a game and wants us to come to him. He won't kill the last of his bait," I interrupt Azi, who looks at the Protectors and then back to me with a long sigh.

"I will go and get wood," Azi finally concedes, walking out of the room without looking back.

"I'm going as well," Nix says and steps close to Connor. "You should come, too. We must bury our royals because they deserve that much." Connor stands up silently and follows Nix and Azi out of the room. Trex and I are silent for a long time, and I only move to put my bag down near the corner of the room, looking in to see Star fast asleep inside. I don't want to wake her as she walked for at least two hours today, and she must be tired. I turn when I hear Trex speak.

"I grew up with Emily and Esther. They used to make me come to their tea parties in their tree-house, when I all I wanted was to be fighting. When my parents were gone, Nix and I were sent to live with the royals. Erica didn't want us there, but Emily and Esther did. They were like sisters to me and Nix," he stops, his voice turning into a growl. "And I failed to protect them."

"You didn't fail. This isn't on you, Trex," I argue.

"Does it take two of my friends being murdered to get you to be nice to me?" he asks, and I know he is changing the subject. He doesn't look at me as he speaks, but I imagine I could see the guilt in his eyes. I can certainly hear the guilt in his voice.

"I may not like you, but I know what it's like to blame yourself for your friend's death. I might as well have killed my guardian, my best friend," I admit, my voice echoing around the dusty room.

"What happened?" he asks quietly. I only tell him because I think he needs the distraction. Because even if he is an asshole, he shouldn't live with this guilt.

"When Hali was born, everyone wanted her dead straight away. She is a death-marked witch, after all. My friend, well, she wouldn't let her daughter die, so she ran away, and I helped her. It was eight years later that my friend came to see me, like she did every year, and that was her fatal mistake. I told her not to come, but she wouldn't listen. The witches found her, and I had to watch, holding Hali, as they drained her magic. They killed her slowly and painfully, and I couldn't stop it. I couldn't help her without risking Hali's life," I say, rushing the last of the words out. The only one that knows this is Hali, because she watched, too. I couldn't make her look away, and she knew we couldn't move to help her mother. We were lucky to be outside, walking back from the pizza place with food, when they attacked.

"I am sorry," he says, and I know he means it from the sincere tone of his voice.

"When they thought she was dead, they left, and I ran to her, holding her as she died. She begged me to help her, to finish her off because of the pain. It killed me to do as she asked, but I told Hali to turn around, and I did it. I couldn't let her suffer, but that has haunted me for as long as I can remember. Don't let this destroy you. Get revenge instead," I tell him. I look at the women, seeing how pretty they are, and how innocent they look. They didn't deserve this.

"Did you ever get revenge for your friend?" he asks, finally pulling his eyes away from the princesses and over to me. I pause for a second, trying to decide if I should tell him, but something in his green eyes makes me want to.

"I get revenge every day that Hali lives. She is destined to kill a royal witch, and there is only one queen of the witches left. The woman who killed my friend. That is Hali's destiny, and I will help her achieve it. That will be my revenge, even if it will take time, now figure out yours," I tell him, and walk out the building to get some wood for the fire. I turn back once and see haunted dark-green eyes watching me until I round the corner.

Chapter Twenty-Six

EVIE

"THAT WON'T BURN, IT'S TOO DAMP. THE ONES over here are better," Connor tells me, stepping out of the shadows with three big logs in his arms. I drop the branch in my hand and follow him over to some branches that are hidden under the trees instead. He is right, they look drier than the ones I was picking up. Connor watches me silently, though he seems to be thinking about something.

"I used to date Esther, when we were young," Connor suddenly tells me, putting his logs down and sitting with his back against the tree as he pulls his bottle of water out. I go to the tree opposite him, sitting down after putting my branches down next to me. I could do with a rest, anyway. We have been building the pyre for the last five hours, and

I'm shattered. Star has enjoyed the rest. She has been running around after Azi and Nix most of the time as they built the main parts of the pyre.

"How long did you date for?" I ask.

"Not long, we were only sixteen, and when Erica found out, she told everyone. It wasn't worth risking us being together after that," he tells me.

"Why wasn't it worth it?" I ask.

"The royals aren't allowed to date until they are married. I would never have been able to marry a royal because in the Protectors, I'm considered low-class," he says, laughing. "Esther and I were never that serious, just kids messing about, really."

"I'm sorry she died, and you had to see her like that," I say. It's not a pleasant way to see anyone dead. Rotting, and their arms all burnt like the princesses' were.

"I'm sorry she didn't survive this; the world needs people like her in it. She was a good woman. She had three farms she bought with her inheritance, and she used to rehome animals in them. The keepers didn't like her helping others, but she did anyway," he says.

"She sounds like a good person," I reply.

"She might have made a good queen. Emily would have, too," he says quietly, and there's a long silence between us as I stare over at him. His gold hair is messy now, no more of the nice style it had when we came here, but I think it brings out his gold eyes more. I like the relaxed look on him. I can't imagine him in the suits the Protectors usually wear.

"So . . . Protectors have low and high classes? Like humans? Rich and poor?" I ask, and he nods, leaning his head back.

"Yes, it's like how humans used to class themselves, but worse in some ways. Blood means everything to Protectors. It determines how strong you are, and most of the time, you are only as strong as your parents," he informs me.

"Why did they choose you to come here, then? I would have thought they would have sent their strongest," I say, and wince. "No offense."

"None taken, because I *am* one of their strongest," he says with a shrug of his shoulders, but he doesn't say it a cocky way. More like just stating a fact.

"Then, I'm confused," I say, making him laugh.

"I'm not one-hundred percent Protector. My father was a reaper," he says, shocking me.

"Reapers don't breed outside their race, and no one knows much about them. It's unheard of that you're half of one," I say, and he nods with a smirk. I try to think about anything I've heard about reapers as I look at Connor, and don't come up with much. Human rumours are all that comes to mind. Reapers are meant to take souls and demons to Hell, but who knows if they do? Protectors take a lot of the demons to Hell these days, so how useful could the reapers be?

"Yeah, I don't know much about my father or my reaper side. I only know I have boosted strength, heighten senses, and I can see some souls on Earth if I'm really close to them. Usually, I can see a person's soul if I witness their death, also," he explains. "It helped me jump up the ranks in Protector academy and leave as one of the top students. Nix, Trex, and the three princesses were the others. We all got pretty close scores."

"Then, maybe the rumours that reapers take lost souls to Hell is true," I say.

"Yeah. I mean, I know some things my mother told me. I don't get to see her for long, and we don't talk of my father much in the little time we have once a week," he smiles sadly. "She told me that my father takes the worst kind of demons back to Hell and manages souls. That's the job of a reaper apparently."

"What do you mean about your mother?" I ask, and he looks away, tightening his jaw.

"She is imprisoned for the rest of her life. She has been in there since I was born, and I was placed in an adoptive home to be watched. Once they realised I wasn't a danger, they let me see her once a week," he tells me, still not looking my way.

"What was she imprisoned for?" I ask.

"Loving my father and keeping me a secret until she was in labour. Mixing Protector's blood with other kinds is illegal to the Protectors. Blood above all else is one of our most important laws," he explains to me.

"Then the Protectors are as evil as I thought they were. Your mother did not deserve a sentence like that simply for falling in love," I bite out as I shake my head in disgust.

"Our kind doesn't make the right decisions all the time, but they make the decisions that keep us safe," he states firmly, and I can tell he believes wholeheartedly in the Protectors, their rules. There isn't much point in arguing with him. I look away, picking up some of the branches and spotting a small, red bunch of flowers.

"Can I ask you something?" Connor asks, and I

look away from the flowers for a second to nod at him. "Who taught you to fight?"

"A demon," I say, not wanting to explain anything more. I pull two of the red flowers out of the ground, and walk over to Connor, placing them in his hand.

"I watched a lot of people being buried in the demon underground. Every weekend, there would be burials of demons or some random person. Every time, they put a plant or flower in their hands. They said the dead should take a little bit of the Earth with them in death as their souls leave their bodies," I say, and he closes his hand over mine on the flowers.

"For a woman people fear, you are the kindest woman I've met in years," he says, staring down at me with those addictive to look at, striking, gold eyes. I know I can't look away, not as he draws me into him. If this was any other place, any other time, and any other person, I'd have his clothes off by now. The simple fact he is off-limits to me, is annoying as well. Everything is gorgeous and irresistible about him.

"I'm not kind, not usually, anyway. I'm downright evil when I'm pissed off," I warn him, and his eyes gleam with humour.

"I'll remember not to piss you off, then," he replies.

"Who says we will even see each other again when all this is over?" I counter.

"We will, because there is no way I'm letting you walk out my life, Blue," he vows, letting go of my hand and keeping the flowers. I don't move as he picks up his logs before walking away, leaving me a little speechless and fearful that Azi might be right. These Protectors are good at breaking my defences down, and that is dangerous for someone like me.

Chapter Twenty-Seven

EVIE

"IT'S TIME TO START," CONNOR SAYS, GENTLY touching Trex and Nix's shoulders as they stand in front of the wood platform. The princesses are resting on top of it, side by side and holding hands. I watched as the Protectors placed them up there, and Connor slid the red flowers into their hands on their chests. Azi stands close to my side, watching silently as Connor steps to my other side. I don't know these people, and it feels wrong to be at their funeral. They should have people who loved them here. At least they have Trex, Nix, and Connor. Azi and I as witnesses.

"Emily Ravenwood and Esther Ravenwood, today we say goodbye to you, and free your souls,"

Trex says, his voice seeming like it's louder than it is, and it echoes around us. "As royal princesses, this is not the death you deserved, and I will forever be sorry that I couldn't save you. As my friends, people who were like sisters to me, I will never forget you. I will never forget your laughs, your kindness, and your beauty. The world never deserved either of you, but we will miss you greatly." Trex looks at Nix, who nods once as Trex finishes his words and looking down before he starts to talk.

"As children, you used to chase me around, telling me my hair was so soft, and that it could be plaited easily. I never did let you catch me, but I remember the night you snuck into my room and plaited it all in my sleep," he holds up a piece of his hair he must have cut off and plaited. He places it on top of the platform, holding his hand over it as he looks up. "You finally got what you wanted. I will miss you both and you will always be remembered. Rest in peace Emily and Esther." With those final words, Trex and Nix step back, and Azi walks over to them, holding a ball of fire in his hand.

"Tell me when," he says quietly, respectfully.

"May death guide you on your way, may angels save your soul, and may you be reborn true. We bless your death in the light of the Protectors who fell before you," Trex says, bowing his head. I've never heard the words before, but for some reason, they feel familiar. I can feel they have some great meaning, something that I didn't quite expect to recognise or connect to, but I do. I know I have Protector blood, I have their runes, but I have never thought of myself as a Protector before. Never had a connection to the people I share my blood with, but for a brief second as Trex speaks, I felt a connection. Nix and Connor repeat the sentence, and I find myself doing the same, quietly, but I know they can hear me. Trex lifts his hand to Azi, signalling him to go ahead, and he holds the ball of fire on the wood, walking around it and setting the entire pyre on fire. We stand still, watching the fire burn, none of us wanting to be the first one to move. Trex is the first one to move in the end, picking his bag up off the floor and looking over at Azi.

"Where are we heading then?" Trex asks.

"It's underground, and nowhere I should take you. Only overlords are meant to go there, but if Roth took your princess there, the rules have already been broken," Azi says, picking his own bag up and walking around the fire to the building. I pull my bag up on my back, hearing Star's light snoring as I follow him. Azi stops, throwing up another fireball into the air as he kneels down to the spot where the princesses were left for us. He places his hand on the ground, into their blood and a red-light flashes once. The floor begins to shake as Azi stands up, stepping back, and part of the floor slides away to reveal a staircase. Azi goes to walk down them, but I grab his arm, stopping him.

"What is down there?" I ask.

"Do you trust me?" he asks, and I pause, staring at him.

"Not with everything, not yet, but are we safe?" I ask quietly, and I let go of his arm.

"Nothing here is safe, but I will never let anything happen to you, Vi," he says tenderly. I don't reply as Azi walks down the steps, with Connor following first, and I go next, hoping I'm not making a mistake by trusting a demon. The steps go down for what seems like forever, and I pull a dagger out as we walk down them. Azi keeps throwing balls of fire into the air around the stair-case, lighting our way. I look at the walls on the way down, noticing drawings and what looks like runes written all over them. I feel a little shift of the staircase under my feet, and then it shakes harshly, knocking me to the floor. The shaking gets worse, and I look down at the cracks in the stone under my hands, just moments before the floor falls in.

Chapter Twenty-Eight

EVIE

I OPEN MY EYES AND SEE NOTHING BUT DUST AND broken stone littered around me. I cough as I suck in some much-needed air and turn my head to the side a little. There are bits of light still left from Azi's fireballs flashing in the room, but I can't see anyone else from where I've fallen. I feel little cuts all over me, but nothing that needs healing right now. The room spins as I push myself up off my chest, pushing broken stone off my legs and back, and I scramble to pull my bag off my back. I open the bag up, and Star jumps out, licking my neck as I check her over.

"You're okay, you landed on me, lucky cat," I sigh in relief, and she purrs in response. I put her down, feeling around for a dagger on my belt, and stand up.

"Azi? Trex? Connor? Nix?" I shout each of their names, but nothing but silence answers me. Something is either seriously wrong, or they are all dead. But that doesn't make sense, Azi could have made a portal to escape and come back for us. *I don't like this.* I look back down at Star and pat my thigh.

"You can follow me or stay here. You choose," I say, and she purrs, settling down next to my bag and sticking her head inside to look for food, I suspect. I turn around in a circle, looking for anything to follow when I hear a slight noise. Like a whimper. I climb over what is left of the staircase, ducking under different bits to get to the other side of the room where I find a door. I pull some of the loose stone in front of the it out of the way, before pulling the door open, and walking into the empty corridor. There are no other doors that I can see, just a long corridor with smooth, stone walls and I can't see the end of them. It's light in here from the little lights in the ceiling which oddly look modern. I'm tempted to shout "hello" like the bimbos in horror movies always do, but I know that won't help. This place is worse than a horror film, it's fucking hell.

"Help me!" a weak-sounding female voice calls from my left. I look at the empty corridor, knowing I should leave the voice alone and walk away, but I don't. I walk left. The corridor is bare of anything as I keep walking and get to the dark end where there is a random door. It's locked when I try the handle, so I step back, lifting my leg and kicking it. It takes three kicks before the door falls through, smashing to the floor. I walk in, pausing at the sight of a woman tied up to a wall on the other side of the room. She looks up, her long black hair covering her face momentarily, and then her blue eyes lock on to me. She only has a simple black dress on, so I can see the runes she has, and I can also see the bruises all over her arms and face. Her legs are covered in dirt, she has blood on her face near the bruises, but she is alive.

"Erica? The princess?" I ask, and she nods her head, smiling widely. I don't even know why I asked, it's clear who she is. She looks just like Emily and Esther.

"You came for me? Who are you?" she asks, her voice nervous and scared. I poke my head back out the door, seeing no one in the corridor before walking back in, and kneeling down next to her.

"My name is Evie," I say, and her eyes widen.

"The deadly assassin? They sent *you* after me?" she asks in surprise, and I nod as I reach for the rope that is tied to a metal loop on the wall. I cut her free, and her arms drop down. I cut the rope off her wrists, acutely aware of her staring at me the whole time.

"What are you staring at?" I finally ask.

"You seem so . . . so human; like you're normal, but you look so much like a Protector," she says, and I give her a confused look as she rubs her wrists, and tries to stand up.

"Being like a human isn't that bad," I say, catching her arm when she sways as she stands.

"I'm weak. The demon has been giving me something that makes me pass out, and I haven't eaten since I was taken," she says, and I switch my dagger to my other arm, putting an arm under hers and holding her up as we walk over the door, and into the corridor.

"Do you know a way out of here?" I ask her as I put my dagger away to hold onto her.

"Yes, down here is a room I was brought through. It has a portal that I saw. I don't know where it leads, but anywhere is better than here. Right?" she asks, and I nod, not knowing what to make of Trex's fiancé. She does seem sweet, he was right. Sweet is the only word I could describe her as. I hold her up as we walk down the corridor and get to the door she mentioned. I let her go, resting her on the wall. I turn the door handle slowly as I slip a dagger out of my belt.

"Stay out here, let me check it out first. Alright?" I ask, and she nods, leaning against the wall and looking exhausted. Let's hope she survives the trip out of here. I need to take at least one princess back, save Hali, and then find the Protectors and Azi. I can't leave them down here without trying to find them. *I've become attached to the fuckers*. I open the door, stepping into the impressive room. I stop a few steps in, realizing something is seriously wrong as I see Azi held unconscious between two men in the middle of the room. I see the unconscious, dirt-covered Protectors all tied up near one of the walls from the corner of my eye, and I'm not sure who to run for first. I gasp as pain shoots through my back, once and then twice. I turn, seeing Erica standing behind me as she pulls the dagger out of my back for the second time. My own dagger falls to the ground as my hands go to my stomach, feeling the blood dripping through my shaking fingers.

"Hello, little sister, thanks for walking straight into my trap," she laughs, and I fall to the ground.

Chapter Twenty-Nine

EVIE

I HOLD IN ANY SOUNDS OF PAIN AS I CLAMP MY hands over my stomach, and lie on the floor, watching my apparent sister step over me and walk to where Azi is being held. The two men holding him are strangers to me, but they look familiar. They look like Azi, and I would bet on them being his brothers. One has black hair that reaches his feet, covering most of his face, and a skinny body in an expensive suit. The other is massive, with a bald head and a face covered in tattoos. He also wears an expensive suit, his eyes never leaving Erica. It's clear he desires her.

"You have done your part, and you have your prize. Leave," she waves a hand at them. They both bow, turning with a still unconscious Azi in their arms, and walk to the back of the room. A flash of light fills the room suddenly, and then they are gone. There must be a portal there. I only need to get to it. There is a silence in the room as Erica just stares at me, and me at her. She is my sister. And that means Emily and Esther were, too. I've always looked for my family, and the first one I find alive, stabs me in the back. Literally. I would laugh, but any movement makes the room spin and pain roll through every part of my body like a wave. Erica pushes her waist-length black hair over her shoulder, picking up a black cloak off the ground and clipping it on. The same cloaks Esther and Emily were buried in. They have the four runes embroidered down the sides. Two on each side. I try to focus on anything else; anything but the pain and the knowledge that I'm going to die. There is no point calling my healing rune, I could never heal this myself. I glance at the dagger near me, wondering if I could just grab it and throw it at Erica. Make her go into death with me.

"Don't even think about it," Erica says, walking over and picking up the dagger. She leans over me, pulling out my purple sword and checking me for any other weapons. I want to fight her off, but when I try to lift my hand, it only shakily moves.

"Erica?" Trex's confused voice carries over to us. I turn my head slightly, the movement shooting pain through me, but I can see Trex as he stares at me. Erica spins my sword in the air, and then throws it across the room.

"That's a piece of crap."

"Like you," I cough out, but she ignores me to turn to Trex. *Bitch.*

"Trex, hunny, I'm so glad you're awake," she says sweetly, and I mentally roll my eyes. Erica is anything but sweet. She is clearly a good fucking liar. Trex looks at her for a second, then his eyes go over to me and widen.

"What the fuck did you do to Evie? She came with us to save you!" Trex shouts, and he stands up, only to find himself unable to move due to the rope tying all of them to the wall behind them. "Why the fuck am I tied up?"

"I will untie you once my sister, Evie, is dead," Erica replies simply, and I hear Trex gasp.

"Your what?" he asks, shaking his head and staring at me. His eyes run over my wounds and back to my eyes.

"Well, seeing as we have a bit of time until she dies, I might as well go over a little royal history lesson," Erica says, spinning the dagger she stabbed me with in her hand. She leans down, tilting her head to the side as she looks at me. I hear Connor waking up, coughing and talking to Trex. His words seem to fade out, and I can only focus on Erica. *The crazy bitch.*

"Our mother was a little bit of a slut once a upon a time, after she had me and my sisters that is. We were perfect, but never enough, and neither was my father, apparently," she says, tutting. "She had an affair, and pop, you were born. We are only a year apart, you know? She didn't wait long to cheat and have a creature like you." I try to listen to her story, only hearing that my mother was the queen of the Protectors, and she had three other children. I had a family and, apparently, my father wasn't the king. *So . . . who was he? And what went wrong, so I ended up on the streets?*

"Lies!" Connor shouts, and Erica laughs, standing up and kicking me in the stomach. The pain almost threatens to make me black out as I roll across the floor and land on my back with a groan. I hear Connor shouting in the distance as Erica walks over and stands above me, looking down in disgust.

"My father left me notes, a note with your name, and where to find you before he died years later. He wanted me to help you, bring you into the family because you are a part of my mother. All I saw was a repulsive secret, and one that needed to be destroyed," she spits out, glaring at me.

"You-you had me hunted all this time because you were jealous? Are you really that fucking crazy?" I ask, coughing and feeling warm blood drip down my cheek. She narrows her eyes at me before kicking me once more in stomach, and I roll across the floor again, facing the Protectors this time and also closer to them.

"Evie! Get up and fight!" I hear and see Nix shout at me. I want to agree, do as he asks, but I can't. Erica leans down right in front of me and places her cold hand on my cheek.

"Dear sister, I've wanted you dead since I was a child. I was ten when I sent the first Protector after you, and they failed. Every single one failed to kill you, and I knew I had to do something before the trials for the new queen started. I couldn't risk fighting you in them, and it was about time you died," she says almost soothingly, like she wants me to agree with her crazy plan.

"You killed your sisters, didn't you?" I manage to wheeze out.

"Our sisters, don't forget, and yes I did. They were smart, fast, and good fighters. I couldn't risk not winning the throne. I need it for the future and what needs to happen," she says, still stroking my cheek. I have a feeling she killed our sisters before they were even kidnapped by her demon friends.

"You fucking bitch, Erica! The keepers will never give you throne when they find out what you did!" Trex growls out, and I hear him struggling against his bindings, trying to escape and help me.

"That's what makes this all perfect, they will never know. Everyone that knows, is here, and will soon be dead or exiled from the Protectors for failing to save their princesses," Erica laughs. She has planned this all, and we have walked straight into her trap. My sister is smart, but it's a shame she is fucking crazy, too.

"We know! And we won't stay quiet. You kill her, Erica, and I swear I will hunt you down and finish you myself," Trex threatens, and I'm surprised to find I believe him. I didn't think the asshole liked me.

"No one would believe you, and you have no proof. Our engagement is over, not that it was anything other than words, anyway," Erica smiles sweetly at an angry-looking Trex, who keeps his eyes on me. Erica looks back down at me as everything goes black in the corners, and the pain starts to disappear into a feeling of emptiness.

"Good bye, sister. Shame you're not the deadly assassin I always feared you would be. You were too easy to kill," she whispers to me with a maniacal grin, and she leans down, stabbing the dagger straight into my heart.

"May death guide you on your way, may angels save your soul, and may you be reborn true. We bless your death in the light of the Protectors who fell before you," I hear all three of my Protectors say with sorrow lacing their words, and then everything fades into darkness.

Chapter Thirty

EVIE

"Evelina, you are so beautiful," I hear a woman say. Her voice is kind, gentle, and reminds me of a distant memory. A memory of a woman speaking to me, singing me a song. I blink my eyes open, seeing a woman floating in front of me. She almost looks like she is in a cloud, her white dress flowing and the cloud surrounding her. She has long black hair, a crown, and four runes marked on her forehead, with swirls dipping down the sides of her eyes. She is stunning, and as her blue eyes meet mine, I just want to know who she is.

"Who are you?" I ask.

"Evelina, I made a mistake, and as a result, you were left alone. I regret every moment of my mistake and now you must pay for it. I can only see you now because death closes in

on you," she replies, ignoring my question, and it's all I can think about instead of her words.

"Who are you?" I repeat.

"Erica is lost in pain, and you must end her. Send her to me," she says.

"Who are you?" I ask again, demanding this time.

"I love you. I loved you from the moment I held you, and you opened your eyes, breaking my heart because you remind me of your father. You were the last thing I thought of as I died. I will always love you, Evelina,"

"Who are you?" I ask once more, but this time my voice cracks, and hot tears fall down my cheeks.

"You already know, but you have to leave," she says sadly, moving closer to me and placing her hand on my chest over my heart. "I'm with you, always."

"Mother?" I ask, and she nods, only seconds before she fades away and I fall through the clouds.

I LIE VERY STILL AS I LOOK UP AT THE LIGHT around me; it is the brightest light that I've ever seen. The light is everywhere, it's soothing and perfect as it warms my skin. Most of me doesn't want to move. Most of me feels nothing but the light for a long time, but then a brief glimpse of a memory comes to me. A man with red eyes. Another man with a cheeky smile, and two brothers with a dark appeal to them. I remember them, and it feels like they are calling to me somehow. I feel like they need me. I sit up suddenly, as everything else flashes through my mind, until I remember the last thing that happened.

I should be dead.

I feel around my chest, noting that I'm completely naked, and find a scar where the dagger went into my heart and my stomach. The scar is white, and there is no blood anywhere on me. My blue hair falls over my shoulders, hiding my chest as I look up at the white skies. They are beautiful.

"Scars are good; they proved you lived," a light, male voice says, and I look over, staring in awe at an angel walks over to me. He has big white wings, white hair, and bright-white eyes. He kneels down close to me, watching me carefully as I gape at his wings as they spread out. His clothes look old, like white rags.

"Are you an angel?" I ask, and he nods.

"Am I dead? Am I in Heaven?" I ask another question, and this time he frowns, shaking his head.

"Angels do not die in Hell. We never have. We become the light," he says like that should explain everything, but it doesn't explain a damn thing.

"I died in Hell . . . this doesn't make any sense," I shake my head, and he sighs.

"You have no idea what you are, do you, Evie?" he asks, and I shake my head again.

"Look behind you, and that is the start of your answers," he says. I turn my head to the side and see long black wings spreading out from my back, hovering in the air. *Wings? I have goddamn wings? What the hell?*

· E p i l o g u e ·

TREX

"You crazy kid! Don't try to bite me, I was only getting the water bottle out of the holder!" Connor shouts, with a pained grunt, and I stop the car in the middle of the highway, resting my head against the wheel. My mind flashes back to seeing Evie lying on the ground, blood pouring out of her stomach onto the floor, and my crazy ex-fiancé holding the knife. Evie was a royal, and I never knew. Evie is who we should have been protecting, and we failed her. I won't fail her witch, though. I look over at Nix, who holds a bottle of whiskey and just stares out of the window, not saying a word. He hasn't said a word since Evie died and oddly enough, her body faded away. It must have been something about dying down there because Erica didn't seem shocked or even to have cared at all. We watched Erica walk through the portal before getting ourselves undone and escaping.

"You kidnapped me! I was waiting for Evie to come back, and I need to be there, or she won't know where to find me! She would never send Protectors after me!" the kid shouts, and I lift my head to see Connor trying to fight her off as she throws her shoe at him. *You can tell Evie brought her up, that's for sure.*

"Kid, listen to me," I say carefully, watching as Star jumps onto Hali's lap, and Connor leans as far away from her as possible. Hali's pale eyes look at me, and all I can see is a scared kid. A scared kid that is acting out. "Evie is gone. I told you this, and I wasn't lying. Now we need to get to safe house, and keep you alive, because it's what she would have wanted. I owe Evie, we all do."

"Evie isn't dead! I know she isn't," Hali cries, looking away and out the window, tears streaming down her face that she harshly wipes away.

"I wish she wasn't dead either, kid, but we don't all get miracles," I say, and start the engine.

Book Two Pre-Order link here.

Thank you so much for reading Runes of Truth!! A big thank you to Michelle, Meagan, Taylor, Amanda and everyone that supported me with this book!

Book two, Runes of Morality, is up on pre-order and this is a trilogy. There is a spin off planned also. Please keep reading for an excerpt from other books of mine, and links on where to find me for updates and teasers!

Thank you and if you have a second, a review would be amazing! They are everything to authors, even if its just a quick "I like this book."

Here are all my links (I love to be stalked so if you have some free time...)-

♥Join my FB Group?♥-

https://www.facebook.com/groups/BaileysPack/

♥Like my FB Page?♥-

https://www.facebook.com/gbaileyauthor/

♥Be my FB friend?♥-

https://www.facebook.com/AuthorG.Bailey

♥Add me on Twitter?♥-

https:twitter.com/gbaileyauthor

🕊Check out my website?🕊-

www.gbaileyauthor.com

♥Follow me on Amazon?♥-

http://amzn.to/2oV9PF5

💜Sign up for my Newsletter?💜-
https://landing.mailerlite.com/webforms/landing/a1f2
v0

ALSO BY G. BAILEY

The King Brothers Series-

Izzy's Beginning (Book one)

Sebastian's Chance (Book two)

Elliot's Secret (Book three)

Harley's Fall (Book Four)

Luke's Revenge (Coming soon)

Her Guardians Series (Complete)-

Winter's Guardian (Book one)

Winter's Kiss (Book two)

Winter's Promise (Book three)

Winter's War (Book Four)

Her Fate Series-

(Her Guardians Series spinoff)

Adelaide's Fate (Coming soon)

Saved by Pirates Series (Complete)-

Escape the sea (Book One)

Love the sea (Book Two)

Save the Sea (Book Three)

One Night series-

Strip for me (Book one)

Live for Me (Coming soon)

The Marked Series (Co-written with Cece Rose)-

Marked by Power (Book one)

Marked by Pain (Book two)

Marked by Destruction (Book Three)

The Forest Pack series-

Run Little Wolf- (Book One)

Run Little Bear- (Book Two)

Protected by Dragons series-

Wings of Ice- (Book One)

Wings of Fire (Book Two)

Wings of Spirit (Book Three)

Wings of Fate (Coming soon)

EXCERPT OF WINGS OF ICE-

Everything inside me screams as I run through the doors of the castle, seeing the dead dragons lining the floors, the view making me sick to my stomach. I try not to look at the spears in their stomachs, the dragonglass that is rare in this world. *Where did they get it?* The more and more bodies I pass, who are both dragon and guards, the less hope I have that my father is okay. *No, I can't be too late, I can't lose him too.* The once grand doors to the throne room are smashed into pieces of stone, in a pile on the floor, and only the hinges to the door still hang on the walls. I run straight over, climbing over the rocks and broken stone. The sight in front of me makes me stop, not believing what I'm seeing but I know it's true.

"Father…" I plead quietly, knowing he won't reply to me. My father is sat on his throne, a sword through his stomach, and a wide mouthed expression on his face. His blood drips down onto the gold floors of the throne room, and snow falls from the broken ceiling onto his face. There's no ice in here, no sign he even tried to fight before he was killed. He must have never saw this coming; he trusted whoever killed him.

"No," is all I can think to say as I fall to my knees, bending my head and looking down at the ground instead of the body of my father. *I couldn't stop this, even after he warned me and risked everything.* I hear footsteps in front of me as I watch my tears drip onto the ground, but I don't look up. I know who it is. I know from the way they smell, my dragon whispers to me their name, but I can't even think it.

"Why?" I ask, even as everything clicks into place. I should have known; I should have never had trusted him.

"Because the curse has to end. Because he was no good for Dragca. Our city needs a true heir, me. I'm the heir of fire and ice, the one the prophecy speaks of, and it's finally time I took what is mine," he says and every word seems to cut straight through my heart. *I trusted him.*

"The curse hasn't ended, I'm still here," I whisper to the dragon in front of me, but I know he could hear my words, as if I had just spoke them into his ear.

"Not for long, not even for a moment longer actually. Your dragon guard will only thank me when you are gone. I didn't want to do this to you, not in the end, but you are too powerful. You are of no use to me anymore, not unless you're gone," he says. I look down at the ground as his words run around my head, and I don't know what to do. I feel lost, powerless and broken in every way possible. There's a piece of the door in front of me that catches my attention, a part with the royal crest on it. The dragon in a circle, a proud, strong dragon. My father's words come back to me, and I know they are all I need to say.

"There's a reason ice dragons hold the throne and have for centuries. There is a reason the royal name Dragice is feared," I say and stand up slowly, wiping my tears away.

"We don't give up and we bow to no one. I'm Isola Dragice, and you will pay for what you have done," I tell him as finally meet his now cruel eyes, before calling my dragon and feeling her take over.

"Isola!" I hear shouted from the stairs, but I keep my headphones on as I stare at my laptop, and pretend I didn't hear her shout my name for the tenth time. The music blasts around my head as I try to focus on the history paper that is due in tomorrow.

"Isola, will you take those things out and listen to me?" Jules shouts at me again, and I pop one of my headphones out as I look up at her. She stands at the end of my bed, her hands on her hips and her glasses branched on the end of her nose. Her long grey hair is up in a tight bun, and she has an old styled dress that looks like flowers threw up on. Jules is my house sitter, or babysitter as I like to call her. I don't think I need a baby sitter at seventeen, not when I'm eighteen in two days anyway, and can look after myself.

"Both headphones out, I want them both out while you listen to me," she says. I knew this was coming. I pull the headphones out and pause the music on my phone.

"I did try to clean up after the party, I swear," I say and she raises her eyebrows.

"How many teenagers did you have in here? Ten? A hundred?" she says and I shrug my shoulders as I sit up on the bed and cross my legs.

"I don't know, it's all a little fuzzy," I reply honestly. My head is still pounding; it was probably the wine, or maybe the tequila shots. *Who knows?* I look up again as she shakes her head at me, speaking a sentence in Spanish that she knows I can't understand, but I doubt it's nice. I don't think I want to hear what she has to say about the party I threw last night anyway. I look around my simple room, seeing the dressing table, the wardrobe, the bed I'm sitting on. There isn't much in here that is personal, no photos or anything that means anything to me.

"Miss Jules, looking as beautiful as always," Jace says, in an overly sweet tone as he walks into my bedroom. He walks straight over to Jules and kisses her cheek, making her giggle. Jace is that typical hot guy, with his white blonde hair and crystal blue eyes. Even my sixty year old house sitter can't be mad at him for long, he can charm just about anyone.

"Don't start with that pouty cute face," she tuts at him and he widens his arms, pretending to be shocked.

"What face? I always look like this," he says and she laughs, any anger she had disappearing.

"I'm going to clean up this state of a house and you should leave, you're going to be late for school. I don't want to have to tell your father that as well, when I tell him about the party," she says, pointing a finger at me, and I have to hold in the urge to laugh. She emails my father all the time about everything I do, but he never responds. He just pays her to keep the house running, and to make sure I don't get into too much trouble. If he hasn't had the time to talk to me in the last ten years, I doubt he's going to have the time to email a human he hired. Jules walks out of the room and Jace leans against the wall, tucking his hands into his pockets. I run my eyes over his tight jeans, his white shirt that has ridden up a little to show his toned stomach and finally to his handsome face that is smirking at me. *He knows exactly what he does to me.*

"You look too sexy when you do that," I comment and he grins.

"Isn't that the point? Now come and give your boyfriend a kiss," he teases, and I fake a sigh before getting up and walking over to him. I lean up, brushing my lips against his cold ones and he smiles, kissing me back just as gently.

"We should go, but I was wondering if you wanted to go to the mountains this weekend and try some flying?" he asks. I blank my expression before walking away from him and towards the mirror hanging on the wall near the door. I smooth my wavy, shoulder length blonde hair down and it just bounces back up, ignoring me. My blue eyes stare back at me, bright and crystal clear. Jace says it's like looking into a mirror when he looks into my eyes, they are so clear. I check out my jeans and tank top, and grab my leather coat from where it hangs on the back of the door before answering Jace.

"I've got a lot of homework to do-" I say and he shakes his head as he cuts me off.

"-Issy, when was the last time you let her out? It's been, what, months?" he asks and I turn away, walking out my bedroom door and hearing him sigh behind me.

"Issy, we can't avoid this forever. Not when we have to go back in two weeks," he reminds me and I stop, leaning my head back against the plain white walls of the corridor.

"I know we have to go back. We have to train to rule a race we know nothing about, just because of who our parents are. Don't you ever want to run away, hide in the human world we have been left in all these years?" I ask, feeling a grumble of anger from my dragon inside my mind. I quickly slam down the barrier between me and my dragon in my head, stopping her from contacting me, no matter how much it hurts me to do so. *I can't let her control me.*

"Issy, we were left here so we would be safe. We are the last ice dragons, and our parents had no choice. Plus… being a dragon around humans is a nightmare, you know that," he says, stepping closer to me.

"I don't want to rule; I don't want anything to do with Dragca," I say, looking away.

"I guess it's lucky we have each other, ruling on our own would have been a disaster," he says, step-

231

ping in front of me so I can't move and gently kissing my forehead.

"I know. I just don't want to go back, to see my father and everything that has to come with it," I say, and he steps back to tilt my head up to look at him.

"You're the heir to the throne of the dragons. You're the princess of Dragca. Your life was never meant to be lived here, with the humans," he says and I move away from him, not replying because I know he sees it differently than I do. He is the ice prince, and his parents call him every week. I haven't spoken to any of my family in ten years and I have never stepped back into Dragca since then. It's the only thing we disagree on, our future.

"Issy, let's just have a good day and then maybe I could get you that peanut bacon sandwich you love from the deli?" he suggests, running to catch up with me on the stairs.

"Now you're talking," I grin at him as he hooks an arm around my waist, and leans down to whisper in my ear,

"And maybe later, I could do that thing with my tongue that you—" he gets cut off when Jules opens the door in front of us, clearing her throat and ushering us out as we laugh.

EXCERPT FROM ESCAPE THE SEA-

I stand on the edge of the cliff, holding the blood-covered crown. The crown we fought so long to get. The crown that will win the war. I glance around at the men I love, each one of them I would die for. My pirates are fighting around me on the battle-field, keeping me alive as I face the king alone. This was always the plan, the only one that would work. The ground shakes as more screams fill the night. I can't look away from the king to see if anyone I know is dying. If anyone I love is.

Everything we have fought for has led us to this moment, and I won't let them down.

We don't say any words to each other, words are not needed. He knew this was coming, and the war around us is proof. The king started this, not me. I was chosen to stop this.

"You will never save the seas," the king sneers at me after a long silence between us.

"I don't need to. The Sea God will save us all," I say, my voice loud as the wind howls, and lightning fills the skies.

"What did you promise him in return?" he shouts back at me. I look the king over, remembering every cruel thing he has done to me, the people he has taken from me, and the deaths he has caused.

"Your death," I say and lift the crown, placing it on my head.

Cassandra

"Name the seven islands of Calais," Miss Drone orders me, like I haven't been taught them my whole life. Every week, she asks me these questions. I will never see any other island than the one I am stuck on, so I don't see the point in knowing all their names.

"Onaya, Twogan, Thron, Foten, Fiaten, Sixa, and Sevten," I answer. *It's like someone has counted to seven, and named an island after each number.*

"Who rules all the islands?" she asks as she reads the paper I wrote for her this week. It's filled with my opinions on the last book she gave me to read, a book about the seven seas.

"King Dragon and his queen, Riah," I answer. I almost want to add that the pirates own the waters, but I know she won't like me saying that. It's not worth the argument that would follow. The king ignores the pirates, and the pirates are said to ignore him. The king chose the seven families to rule each island after he took his throne, then he left us alone on the islands. We only see the king once a year when he visits all the islands with his queen. Well, I've never seen him, his queen, or his children. Only the seven council members get to see them.

There's only one law the king regularly reminds everyone to follow: kill the changed ones, or he sends his guards to the island and kills them anyway.

"Tell me the final words you need to know," she asks in her cold tone.

"Never go near the sea, never leave the walls. The sea is lost, pirates are death," I repeat back to my teacher. Miss Drone believes telling me the same thing every time I see her will make sure I understand her. She really has no idea. She nods like she thinks she's done her job today. Those are always the words she says last to me, every week at the same time, the same hour. The same senseless rules.

My whole life is full of rules that mean nothing to me.

"Cassandra, are you listening to me?" Miss Drone asks in a sharp tone. I glance up from my seat, looking at her. I don't know her first name. She never told me, and I never asked anyone to tell me. My father always calls her Miss Drone, and her daughter calls her Mother. Miss Drone has light-blonde hair that's cut short, and she's wearing an old dress, covered in holes. She is a widow from the poor side of the island. My father says she's lucky, lucky not to be dead or on the streets, and that's why she doesn't tell anyone about me. That's why she has taught me my whole life for the tiny amount of food my father gives her. I guess it's because food is treasured here on Onaya, where we have little. People can't leave, because the seas are full of pirates, and even if you did get to the other islands, they are in no better condition. No one can trade between the islands. The only way we know people are even alive on them is by talking to the couple of people who make it to our shore. They come looking for a home and food, but are sadly disap-pointed. We grow very little on our farms; the land is dying, and people don't know why. It's said to be like this on every island, and it gets worse every single year.

"Yes, of course I am," I say. I fake a smile at her, and she relaxes in her seat. Miss Drone is terrified of me. Everyone that has ever been near me is. My father has only let me meet three people in my life. Him, Miss Drone, and her daughter, Everly. Everly keeps me from going insane with boredom, and Miss Drone teaches me things I apparently need to know. Like how the seas are lost, and everyone dies out there.

I don't know why I need to know anything when I can never leave my house, or the grounds surrounding it.

"Well then, I will be off. Everly will be over after school," she says as she stands and walks towards the door. I wait until she shuts it before I walk towards the window.

I can see my whole town from this window. It's striking. The island is shaped like a foot, or that's how I like to think of it. The brown state house stretches like a line straight down the middle, towards my large house and the large acre that surrounds it. Our house is the biggest on the island because of who my father is—one of seven council members. They always get the best of everything.

There are three others houses on my row, but they are far smaller. I have been told there are three more on the other side of the island, too, the same size as the smaller ones next to ours. I don't know why my father has the biggest house on the island, but he does. I only know what my father has told me. I know that they house the other council members and their families. The council makes all the decisions on the island, everything from enforcing the laws, to how much food they think people need to eat.

The people worship them and do anything they ask, because they give them food. They keep them safe and make sure that no pirates get into their town.

If only they knew about me, his secret, they wouldn't love him like they do. My reflection shines back at me from the window. My brown hair is in waves around my face, with little feathers braided in and tiny plaits I've added when I've gotten bored. My hazel eyes match my hair, in my opinion making me look normal. The only thing that isn't normal is the upside-down, black triangle on my forehead.

My mark; the very thing that makes me hide. The very thing I wish I could get rid of, so I could have a normal life. A life where I could walk out of the house.

"Cassandra, come here," my father shouts up the stairs.

After one more glance at my reflection, I leave my room.